THE LAST HONEYMOON

PAULO GARNSEY

Pacy Books

First published in Australia in 2023 by Pacific Ability

Copyright © P.A. Garnsey 2021
The moral right of the author has been asserted.

Paperback ISBN: 978-0-6459677-0-8
Ebook ISBN: 978-0-6459677-1-5

Typeset in Times New Roman
Printed by Ingram Sparks

Pacy Books is an imprint of Pacific Ability
PO 150 NORFOLK ISLAND NSW 2899
paulgarnsey@gmail.com

TABLE OF CONTENTS

CHAPTER ONE

PLANE

They sat next to each other in the plane. Annie, by the window, but not looking down at the Pacific Ocean eight kilometres below. Mitch, in seat 7B, but not watching the in-flight entertainment on the headrest in front.

They just stared at each other. Studied each other's hands, and eyes, and cheeks, and mouths – in wonder.

Annie's soft hand was in Mitch's not-quite-as-soft hand. She raised it and kissed it, "Hello there, Mr Adams. I'm Mrs Adams."

Mitch raised Annie's hand and kissed it, too, and said, "Why hello there, Mrs Adams. I'm Mr Adams."

Then they chuckled and snuggled into one another.

Glistening young newlyweds with the world at their feet, zooming into a bright blue future at 800 km/h. So much in love, they were almost glowing.

If it was a Disney movie, there'd be animated blue and pink lovebirds tweeting above their heads, possibly braiding Annie's hair. But this ain't Disney. And the biosecurity complexities of animated bird life on an international flight are well beyond the remit of the small Australian Border

Force at Norfolk Island Airport. They'll be struggling with plenty of other problems when the plane lands in 20 minutes.

So, there's no bird life – animated or otherwise – above our newlyweds. Just warm pink hues emanating from their heart chakras.

This is the first time since their wedding last night that Mitch and Annie have stopped whispering and tittering about the ceremony, and the guests, and the hors d'oeuvres, and the first kiss, and the band, and the venue, and Mrs Tanner's unfortunate dress, and Sam's drunken speech … and their main topic of interest – love.

But they'll start on that again, soon.

How warm it is. How pink it is. How bold it is. How lucky they are. How sweet it is. How it's just like all the love songs, but more so.

Mitch started, "None of them quite got it right, did they?"

"You'd think just by the sheer number of love songs," said Annie, "you'd think someone would've stumbled onto it."

And by "it" she meant the soul-scape of love's heavenly terrain that they currently inhabit. Far beyond the ozone and the upper atmosphere of earthly delights. Far into the extra-terrestrial infinity where Mr and Mrs Adams now know true love truly dwells.

Mitch whispered, "Maybe Nat King Cole got close with 'Stardust'."

Annie whispered, "Or Frank with 'Fly Me to the Moon'."

"Or The Beastie Boys with 'Intergalactic'," laughed Mitch.

"Good one," said Annie. "Or Lou with 'Satellite of Love'."

"Bowie's probably closest."

"Of course, he is," said Annie.

" 'Space Oddity'," suggested Mitch.

"I thought you were going to say, 'Starman'," said Annie.

"Or, 'Moonage Daydream'."

"Or, 'Life on Mars'."

"Bowie's definitely closest," said Mitch. "But—"

"But, yeah—" said Annie. "But, nah."

They laughed because even Bowie, even "The Man Who Sold the World" and "The Man Who Fell to Earth", even "Ziggy Stardust and the Spiders from Mars", even the man who wrote "Soul Love" and, even David frickin' Bowie was too limited for the love of Mr and Mrs Adams.

For Mr and Mrs Adams, their love is beyond this known universe. Their love is an alien.

And not one of those two-legged, air-breathing, anthropomorphic aliens of *Dr Who* and *Star Wars*. No, we're talking ethereal astrapods, travelling at the speed of thought, and shooting stars, and gardening galaxies, and big-banging babies as large as our solar system. Invisible, infinite, love beings. Like real aliens are.

"That's how real love is," said Mitch. "That's how our love is."

"And just like real aliens," said Annie, "real aliens, which we know—with the millions of solar systems like our milky way—there must *obviously* be."

"Obviously," said Mitch.

"Well, just like that," whispered Annie, "before I met you, I knew there must be a soulmate for me. That real love must exist somewhere out there."

"And here I am," said Mitch.

"Here you are," smiled Annie.

And they kissed a soft wet kiss.

"But I used to imagine, when I was by myself, sometimes even when I was looking up at the stars—" said Annie.

"Or when I was doing accounting ledgers for clients," said Mitch.

"Oh, did you?" said Annie. "Oh, good," and she paused and was about to kiss him but held back with physical restraint on her features, and said, "but let me finish my thought, while I can still grasp it."

"Of course."

"But even then, when I was hoping it was real—hoping someone was out there for me—when I was a lonely little stargazer in a flat lonely paddock in the middle of outback Queensland, I couldn't have imagined anyone as good as you. And couldn't have imagined how good true love really could be."

"Just like the songwriters and the sci-fi guys—their imagination is too limited."

"Too *bound* by gravity."

"Yes," said Mitch. "Or maybe no one has ever felt like this before."

"Oh, Mitch, surely someone, sometime, in human history."

"I don't know. I just know I feel it. And I ain't ever gonna let it go."

And their soft hands grasped each other's tighter. And they kissed a side-by-side, angled kiss that would've been uncomfortable for mere mortals but was effortless for these two Love Aliens.

Just then, the flight attendant came on the plane's PA: "Flight attendants and cabin crew, please be seated," followed by "ladies and gentlemen, the fasten seatbelt sign has been turned on. The captain has informed us that we can expect some turbulence as we approach Norfolk Island. Please make sure your seat backs and tray tables are in their full upright position and that your seat belt is correctly fastened. We will be landing in about ten minutes. Thank you."

CHAPTER TWO

LANDING

Norfolk Island's a very small, very green island in the middle of the very enormous, very blue Pacific Ocean.

It's a lonely bump of basalt that sticks up above the endless swells of the surrounding sea. Covered in grass, Norfolk Island Pines, cows, and even a few people, the bump is only eight kilometres long and five kilometres wide, but it's 900 kilometres from the next dry land.

Way out there, where the deepest ocean meets the limitless sky, there's all kinds of weather that the rest of the world never sees.

Meteorological anomalies sweep over that lonely bump of basalt, tilting the lush grass, swirling the pines, drenching the cows, and freezing the fishermen.

Sometimes, big, lonely clouds float across that infinite blue sky, pausing above the island for a break. They just sit there like a broody hen on an egg. It feels like you're under a Big Top marquee at a rock festival when it gets so hot and humid that it sucks the moisture out of the writhing dancers and forms enough condensation on the tent ceiling that the sweat rains back down onto the mosh pit below.

Other times, the southerly winds shoot off the Antarctic ice sheets, and blow northwards, straight up between New Zealand and Australia, targeting Norfolk Island like a bulls-eye, with arrows of icicle-rain fired from 6,000 kilometres away.

But most of the time, the Pacific lives up to its peaceful name. The ocean rollers rise and fall – a breathing meditation. The sky is baby blue and the clouds are puffy white, like a mural in a toddler's bedroom. And the sun is loving on Norfolk Island, like the sparkling eyes of a doting mother.

Unfortunately, for our Love Aliens, Annie in 7A and Mitch in 7B, the weather they were flying into was a combination of the first two meteorological anomalies – something like an icicle-targeted mosh pit.

The effect on their 737 aircraft was spectacular.

That's what they called it on the internet: "Spectacular Plane Landing" #StormLanding #NorfolkIsland #CrazyPlanes.

The footage was filmed by a baggage handler on his phone as he stood near the cargo shed at Norfolk Island airport. He posted on the socials under the name #DarrenTheBaron.

"Spectacular" isn't how they described the feeling from inside the plane. *Their* descriptions were much more colourful.

The torrents flowing from their screaming mouths weren't phrases of nouns and adjectives. They were streams of bile, punctuated with tomato skins and coffee-coloured crackers and chunks of the breakfast burrito that'd been served an hour earlier.

Most of this colourful language missed the airsick bags at which it was aimed and flew – or "projected" to use the proper term – onto the fold-down table. And onto the TV screen inset into the seat back. And into the hair of the person sitting in front. And onto the ceiling, from where it rained straight back down on the vomiter and contin-ued to drip, slowly – like condensation raining in the mosh pit – onto the head of the regurgitator. Who, it must be said, couldn't care as they were otherwise occupied, con-centrating on holding the useless bag, or swearing another scream of reconstituted airline food into the airborne cock-tail swishing around inside the cabin.

You know how a toddler holds a toy and suddenly waves it excitedly up and down? That's what God was doing to that 737 airplane.

Fortunately, it didn't break.

By some miracle, the vomit-encrusted captain managed to land his jolting airframe on the small Norfolk Island run-way on the second pass – the last one before his only other option was to abort and head back to Brisbane. Two hours away.

When the plane finally slowed on the tarmac, and tax-ied towards the terminal, there was the briefest relief inside the cabin. The pale-faced, rainbow-clothed passengers sud-denly realised they weren't going to die. Then, the smell made some want to.

Most passengers kept their eyes lowered as they exited the plane. Partly to step over the puddles of vomit. But mainly to avoid eye-contact with their fellow travellers.

CHAPTER THREE

CAR

There was never a quicker clearance of a plane load of passengers through any international airport. An airport as small as Norfolk Island's usually takes a while to screen arrivals. Even though it's an Australian territory and most of the passengers are Australian, it's still an international flight with strict biosecurity border controls, especially for wildlife.

But as soon as the automatic doors from the tarmac slid open to the Arrivals Hall, the stench of the arriving passengers wafted towards the Customs and Border Force staff, who were waiting to process them. Usually a highly sought-after job on the island, today these brave first responders looked at each other with raised eyebrows and pinched noses, like they wanted to be anywhere else. Then they collectively shrugged, straightened their spines and held their breaths, stoically facing the oncoming swarm.

This stoicism lasted all the way until the small hall was filled to capacity, veritably choking with soiled passengers, and the auto doors had closed them all in. The first passengers had collected their crumpled baggage and were standing at the small immigration counter. The officers had their masks up while pinching their noses and talking like they had colds.

Customs officer: "Barsport, blease."

Passenger: "Passport?"

The Customs officer nodded.

"Oh, yes, of course," said the passenger, not realising they'd need to show it to gain entry from Australia into Australia. They'd rifle through their carry-on luggage as the agent dry-retched.

To move the stench along, her Customs colleague stood up on the resting rung of his chair, and shouted into the melee, "Blease have your bassports ready."

Then he sat down and gasped at the pungent elderly man smiling in front of him. He had his passport on show and vomit on his cheek. The Customs agent waved him past and stood again on the rung of his chair, and shouted, "Just bresent your bassport for biewing. Keep moving."

"Quickly now," he said, waving people past, until he met our newlywed couple. Annie was slicking Mitch's hair back with vomit.

"Honeymooners?" the agent laughed, but just as quickly dry-retched again, closed his eyes and waved them past. After that he just kept his head down, eyes closed, and continued impatiently waving for people to pass.

Outside, holidaymakers rushed out of the small tropical terminal. And just as quickly, their loved-ones, family members, tour guides, and friends who were waiting to welcome them, recoiled from the smell.

Mitch and Annie pulled their three bags into the bright sunshine of the now, perfectly clear, blue-sky day. Both immediately saluted to shield their eyes as they took in the beautiful trees and green hills beyond the airport fence. They started looking for their names on the "welcome" boards held by greeters,. They walked through assembling tour groups with their suitcases, and past the guides with their clipboards and name badges, all the way to the car park, which was full of small buses and shiny hire cars.

There were drivers in hibiscus-print shirts helping passengers in their vomit-stained ones into tour buses. There were young families towing the crumpled luggage of their crumpled parents. There was a priest sitting with a baggage handler on a tractor towing a luggage trailer, laughing loudly at something on the baggage handler's phone. But there were no name boards with any version of "Mr and Mrs Adams".

Mitch and Annie looked around the car park and walked back through the muddle of greeters again. They looked around and around, like sad lighthouses, but all they saw were the other passengers disappearing into buses and rental cars.

Only when the last tour bus left, and the baggage tractor rumbled away – driven by #DarrenTheBaron – only then did the priest finally turn his sign around to display "Mr and Mrs Adams".

Mitch and Annie sighed and shook their heads, then smiled at each other and their eyes shone together because such petty annoyances are like water off a duck's back for Love Aliens. They pulled their luggage over to the priest, and said, "We're the Adamses."

"Oh, there you are," said the priest. "I was starting to get worried."

Mitch started to say, "Your sign was—" but Annie put her arm around his shoulders, and they shot love to one another's eyes, and Annie finished the sentence, "—hard to find."

"Eyes just for each other, eh," said the priest. "You must be honeymooners."

Annie said, "How did you know?"

"I've seen my fair share of newlyweds," said the priest, "but not many covered in as much puke you two."

The couple appraised each other with bright eyes.

"A few," said the priest, "but not many."

They laughed.

"Come on," said the priest, "I'll take you to your car and you can go home and clean up."

Mitch asked, "You're the rent-a-car guy?"

"Yep. Everyone has a couple of jobs on Norfolk," said the priest. "I'm the local priest, the rent-a-car guy – as you so aptly named it – and I'm one of the announcers on the local radio station. I also do some cleaning with the wife who teaches at the school and drives a tour bus." He continued to explain island employment as they walked across the car park to a shiny blue Subaru SUV.

"Keys are already in it," said the priest. "Just leave 'em in there, too. Everyone does."

Annie asked, "Everyone leaves their keys in their car?"

Mitch said, "That's very trusting."

"Well, yes," said the priest, "but also, if someone stole it there'd be nowhere to take it. The island's so small, someone's gonna see it."

Mitch laughed, "They can't really drive it to the next town and sell it, can they!"

"No," agreed Annie. "It looks like a good car, but I doubt it'd float."

"No, it doesn't float," said the priest, "so don't try."

The Love Aliens smiled at the strangeness of Earth people, then shook their heads at each other to say, "They just don't get our 'love galaxy' humour."

The priest asked where they were staying and whistled when they told him the name, "Ooh very nice. 'On Dar Cliff'. Some young people like starting their honeymoon fancy. Not me of course."

Annie asked, "Why?" But the priest was pointing across the car park at a rusty white truck, and saying, "That's me there. So just follow me." As he walked he turned to say, "Oh, one thing. Cows have right of way on Norfolk Island."

"Cows?"

"Yes, it's called the long paddock, the whole of Norfolk is their pasture. You'll see 'em everywhere," said the priest as he turned away towards his car.

The Love Aliens smiled at each other, loving this enchanted land where they'd landed.

They got into their car where the key was in the ignition. Then the priest drove up next to them and stuck his head out the window.

"And don't worry about people waving at you. It's the Norfolk way. Everyone waves at every other driver. Just wave back."

Sure enough, as they followed the priest's beaten-up jalopy at 30 km/hour along the wide main street, between cafés, tour operators' offices and small boutiques, Mitch and Annie squirmed with childish delight as they returned the waves of every passing car.

On the radio a song finished; the announcer said it was KC and the Sunshine Band and then played a Radio Norfolk jingle in which an old lady said in a delightful Norf'k singsong accent, "There's no sutch theng as gawssep orn Norf'k Aislen. Ony noos."

Annie said, "I love this place."

"Me, too," said Mitch.

The shops thinned out and the road became rougher and full of potholes. The few residential palings gave way to country post-and-wire fences stretched across lime-green paddocks dotted with cows. The lush hills dipped into valleys of pine forests and rose again to views of the azure sea sparkling with sunlight, and the clean horizon floating on its farthest edge.

"There's the ocean," said Annie excitedly.

Then the potted road curved back on itself, and Annie pointed and said again, "There's the ocean, there, too."

"It's like it's all around us," said Mitch.

Annie scoffed and slapped his shoulder. "Of course, smart-arse, but it's amazing how small the island is. We can see the water from everywhere."

Mitch smiled. Annie took his photo, then pointed her phone out the window at cows on the roadside. "Oh, cows," said Annie. "Can we stop and pat them?"

"Later," said Mitch, "but now we have to follow the rent-a-car priest." So, they just waved at the cows and kept driving. None of the cows waved back.

Annie swivelled her phone left and right, and took photos, saying, "Look at that" and "Oh my God! So beautiful."

Mitch swivelled his head, smiled sublimely, and opened his blue eyes wider just to take in the dramatic beauty.

A cow stepped out in front of their car.

And just like that, they carved straight into it. To say they butchered it would be a cheap pun. To say the cow slaughtered the Subaru SUV would be carma. Let's just call it carnage and be done with it.

It was all over in three horrendous seconds. The crumpled car was in the ditch with the cow embedded in the front windscreen; her four legs and head of the cow poking up in the air over the bonnet. There was one pure second of absolute silence. Then the world crashed in.

First, the song on the radio, "Everyone's a Winner" by Hot Chocolate.

Then the song of voices.

Most impressively, Annie, with the cow's neck pressing against her forehead let out a blood-curdling scream from a depth of trauma none could've imagined the beautiful young woman possessed.

Mitch was muffled by the weighty rump of a prime Norfolk Blue heifer, but made up for his lack of volume with the perfect pitch of his physical agony. You knew instinctively, from his groaned baritone, this man was in true pain.

Then came the throaty bellow of the cow. She started from the lower bass tones of all four stomachs and rose into a shrieking soprano that spoke of fear and pain in any language.

The next vocals were the harmony of wailing from the two owners of the cow, a mother and daughter who'd been tending a calf nearby when the accident happened. It was shrieking sadness and shock, but in a tragic way their screams sounded sweet. They say some family members make perfect duets because of the genetic similarities of jaw shape, vocal cords, and dental anatomy. And the power of these combined voices carried that sad sweet sound across the green valleys of Norfolk Island.

"Mildred—" they wailed in unison.

The final voice was from the calf that the women had been tending. Instinctively linked to its mother, who was bellowing in pain, this young baby cried a mewling drone that gutted the tenor range and was so horribly tragic it was impossible to hear without crying for one's own mother.

Altogether it was a four-part harmony from hell. All it needed was violin – the saddest of all instruments – to make it the most sorrowful song ever heard. And soon the violin part was filled by the abrasive siren song of the approaching ambulance.

What ensued was a long and tawdry affair that included fiery tempers, searing tears, and spittled accusations of negligence from both sides.

Within minutes and seemingly out of nowhere, the road was cluttered with vehicles. The scene was a havoc of farmers, council workers, and fishermen all heaving and shouting directions to pull Mildred out of the front window of the rental car, while the two ambulance men tried to open the buckled car doors.

Inside the car was entirely red. The gashes to the cow's back and rear as she smashed through the windscreen had gushed a torrent of blood throughout the car. Most noticeably onto the inhabitants, Mitch and Annie.

The ambulance drivers, Greg and Steve, were talking to Annie and Mitch inside the car while trying to open the doors to free them from the car. Everyone else was trying to dislodge Mildred from the window. There was a rope around her neck and her legs, which was attached to the tractor in the adjacent paddock.

The tractor was towing, the cow was bellowing, hands were tugging, and voices were shouting for Annie and Mitch to "Push... push" Mildred from inside the car. They did, and it worked.

Very slowly, Mildred's top end was freed from the window. Then very quickly her bottom end freed a lumpy stream of manure straight into the car. Most noticeably onto the inhabitants, Mitch and Annie.

When the newlyweds were finally pulled from the car, they smelt worse than they looked. And they looked terrifying. In fact, two-tone terrifying: Blood red on the top half, and shit-brown on their bottom halves. But miraculously they suffered no serious injuries.

The same couldn't be said for the cow or the car. Mildred, the prime Norfolk Blue heifer, had an injured front leg and couldn't stand properly. Candice, the vet, was already bandaging the leg beside the road and would know after some tests back at the clinic whether Mildred would survive.

The shiny new Subaru SUV didn't need tests to tell you it was a complete write-off.

"Fortunately, it's covered by insurance,' said Father Pat, the rent-a-car priest. Then, looking at his watch said, "Eleven minutes. That's the quickest insurance claim I've ever seen. But you'll still have to pay the excess of eighteen-hundred dollars."

Mitch and Annie looked at each other's blood-soaked faces, in utter desperation. Tears streamed clear lines down Annie's red cheeks. Mitch hugged her tightly - their wet clothes making a farting sound as they held each other. But no one giggled.

"The bad news is," said Father Pat, "there's no other hire cars available on the island."

"Oh, *that's* the bad news," mumbled Mitch into Annie's sticky wet hair. Annie laughed despite herself.

"It's the silly season," said Father Pat, as if that explained everything. "But I can give you a lift to your place after you've straightened it out with the Christians."

"The Christians?" asked Annie.

"Yep," said Father Pat. "Very old family, descended from Fletcher."

"Oh," said Mitch, "Christian's their *name*."

"Yes, what did you think—" asked Father Pat, "Oh, yes—I can see how that'd be confusing."

"Especially cos you're a priest," said Annie.

"Yes," said Father Pat, "And their name is Christian—but it's not their Christian names."

"Oh, what're their Christian names—" said Annie. Then, reconsidering, added, "Actually, I can't do this now, sorry Pat."

They walked slowly over to the two women keening over their cow. Father Pat introduced the two grieving farmers, Smiley and Polly Christian.

It wasn't a laugh fest. Especially when Mitch tried to explain to the farmers, "I'm sorry, it just jumped out."

"Oh, yeah," said Smiley, the mother. "We're famous for our jumping cow breed."

"Oh yeah," said Polly, the daughter, "blame the cow, why don't you." Which actually made Father Pat spurt laughter, but he immediately pulled it in and covered his mouth.

Mother said to daughter, "Your dad will be heartbroken." And the women hugged each other crying.

Father Pat took this cue to lead the newlyweds away from the accident to the back of the ambulance.

The only benefit from the incident was that the blood-drenched couple were no longer concerned about being covered in vomit.

The paramedics, Steve and Greg, cleaned a mask of blood from Annie and Mitch's faces with saline spray and swabs, while searching for wounds. Miraculously, there were only a few tiny scratches, even though they looked like they'd stepped out of the prom scene from *Carrie*.

Annie sat in stoic silence while the ambo tended her scratches. The only physical effects of the accident were her hands quivering in her lap.

Mitch complained of slight neck pain but was otherwise unscathed. Greg, the ambo, wrapped a brace around Mitch's neck, just in case, and told them to report to the doctor in two days.

Covered in bright red blood and shit-brown shit from head to foot, except for a beaming circle of clean white on their faces, the honeymooners resembled an horrific vaudeville act when they were released by the ambos and followed Father Pat to his truck.

Worse still, they had to sit in the tray of his truck, where they wobbled like a pair of red rag dolls from some disturbing children's show. Any passer-by would assume this B-grade blood fest was a mistimed Halloween debacle. People used to say Norfolk Island was for newlyweds and nearly deads. Annie and Mitch looked like they had a foot in both camps.

Worse, worse still, Father Pat's white Maltese Terrier, Fuzzy, was also in the back of the truck and kept trying to lick them. So the nearly-dead newlyweds spent the entire trip pushing little white Fuzzy away.

Worst still, Father Pat took them to the ATM in the main street of the small township, to withdraw the excess for the insurance. In Father Pat's favour, he had little choice of venue as it's the only ATM on Norfolk Island.

"Better we get the excess now so we can get everything cleared away," he huffed.

"Now?" said Mitch, incredulous.

"Not everyone's as honourable as you two," said the priest. "People here have been burnt before by tourists who skip their responsibilities and leave the island."

"But that's all our money for the honeymoon," whispered Annie trying to attract as little attention as possible.

"Ahh, your honeymoon," said the priest. "I envy you; you know?"

"What!" scoffed Mitch.

"Most couples think it has to be perfect. But not you two. You've gone straight in there," punching his fist into his palm, "taking on life together, head on." Then he laughed. "Head on! Sorry, I didn't mean it like that. You know ... like a crash?" Then looking from one blank white face to the other, he stopped his laughter, "Sorry."

Mitch looked at Annie and gently touched her fingers. Then he got out of the ute and marched over to the ATM, leaving bloody shit-stains on the footpath, and withdrew $1,800. He gave the wad of notes to the priest in the front of the truck and hoicked himself into the tray with his wife, where he showed her the balance statement of $94.

"Christians!" Mitch said, "Jesus!"

"Are you talking about the priest or the farmers?" asked Annie.

"On this occasion, the priest," said Mitch, "But that could change if that cow dies."

They drove along the main street, painfully aware of the horrified stares they were attracting. The little truck sped up as the road rose over the first green hill. Mitch's eyes widened at the bright green fields, and he said, "So that cow was a Christian cow, eh?"

"I guess so," said Annie.

"You'd think cows would be Hindus," said Mitch. "Better benefits."

Annie laughed then pointed to the healthy cows grazing on the pastures, "I think the cows around here get treated pretty well." Then she glanced back at Mitch and raised an eyebrow, "Well until they meet us on the road."

They groaned guiltily, then Annie shook her head and said, "Sorry." They smiled at each other. Annie asked, "Are we terrible humans?"

"No, not terrible," said Mitch, "but we're definitely humans."

They smiled sadly with self-knowledge as they bumped along the country road while trying to push the dog away. Eventually, glancing at each other and shrugging, they both gave up fending off, Fuzzy, the dog.

"Let him have it," said Annie.

CHAPTER FOUR

HOUSE

Mitch, Annie and Fuzzy - the once white, now red, little dog - slid around the tray as it bumped along country roads that curved through vibrant green pastures. The little truck climbed hills that offered them spectacular views of enormous expanses of Pacific blue ocean. Then it rode down into shadowed valleys where the road was covered in an archway of trees. Annie and Mitch looked up at the blurred green canopy whizzing overhead.

They turned into a dirt driveway that threaded through a forest, weaved up a hill, and stopped at a house on the edge of a cliff overlooking the ocean.

Neither Annie nor Mitch could take their eyes off the view; they climbed out of Father Pat's truck in a trance.

"This is beautiful," said Annie.

"Yep," said the priest, "Sometimes Norf'k language isn't very different from English. And 'On Dar Cliff' is exactly what it is."

"Stunning," said Mitch.

They retrieved their suitcases, thanked Pat, patted Fuzzy, and waved goodbye to the retreating truck. Then they laughed at each other and ran around to the cliff-side of the house. There was a pool and a deck decorated with nautical memorabilia – big old ropes, harpoons, buoys. Beyond that, the two blue view.

Sea blue and sky blue.

Divided into two halves by the slightly bowed horizon line. The light blue above, the navy blue below, and the awesome curvature of the earth between.

The sea immediately connected them with a deep inner calm. The sun high in front of them reflected a silver path across the ocean surface. Like they could step straight out onto it and walk directly to the blade-edged horizon. Puffy clouds in the baby-blue sky reflected white smudges on the top of the navy-blue sea.

Looking down the cliff in front of them, they saw the jagged rock face descend 100 vertical metres to huge black boulders being smashed by white waves. A red-tailed tropicbird floated in the air like a kite against the breeze. Two small Arctic terns sliced across the blue in a sharp white blur of visible wind.

They saw crystal clear rockpools further along the coast. Even from this height they could see the colours of the corals within. And way down there, four yellow kayaks were contrasted against the foreshore basalt.

"This is more like it," said Mitch.

"I think this is the most beautiful place I've ever seen," replied Annie.

They stood arm-in-arm, entranced by the view. Annie snuggled closer to Mitch, and Mitch moved his head closer to her hair, and said, "Oh! no!"

"What?" asked Annie.

Mitch laughed, "We stink."

"Can't go in the pool," said Annie. "It'll turn into a bloodbath."

Mitch looked around and noticed a showerhead hanging off a weathered post.

"Shower!"

They moved to the outdoor shower, stripped, and washed the blood and vomit from each other's body. When they were as clean as they could get, they ran across the deck and dived into the pool.

They surfaced and smiled at each other's beautiful faces and swam closer and kissed.

"I love you," said Mitch.

"I love you more," said Annie.

"Impossible," said Mitch.

They laughed and moved together in a long kiss. They cavorted with the sun beating down on their warm bodies in the cool pool. They got out dripping wet and kissed on the deck overlooking one of the most beautiful views in the South Pacific.

Annie embraced Mitch, who lifted her up, and she wrapped her legs around him. They kissed like that. He grew hard; she lifted and arched.

Then she whispered into his ear, "No, I want to see the view, too."

She got down, turned around and leaned against the wooden railing of the deck. Mitch leaned into her, and they watched the undulating ocean swell rhythmically. The waves smashed against the rocks, and the lovers watched the big boulders emerge and descend in the swirling white-wash. They focused together on the peaceful blue surface of the deepest ocean in the world, moving together with the magic of nature.

They swayed to the sound of the waves crashing, and the wind whistling, and birds whistling, and a shrill man screaming,

"What the hell are you doing?!"

Annie and Mitch turned together to see a family of four standing at the top of the path to the cliff. All were wearing caps, board shorts, towels, and eyes almost as wide as their gaping mouths.

"What the hell are you doing?" shrieked the woman.

"Uhm," said Mitch and Annie as they fumbled, and moved away from each other. Then, the lovers clasped each other and dived back into the pool.

When they surfaced, they looked at the family again; the mother had wrapped the children's towels around their eyes, although the boy was peeking.

"Sorry," said Annie. "We're on our honeymoon."

"Well," said the woman. "Do it somewhere else."

Mitch said, "We're staying here. And this—"

"Like hell you are," said the man. "This is private property."

"Not private enough," said Annie.

"How dare you!" said the mother.

"Are you the owners?" asked Mitch.

"No," said the father. "We've rented it through Airbnb."

"So did we," said Mitch.

Annie: "Oh, no. Have we got the wrong address?"

The woman barked, "Yes. You. Have."

Mitch got out of the pool, crouching over his genitals. Then, shielding his butt-crack, he turtled towards his day-pack. He aimed his bum away from the family and rifled through the bag, one-handed.

The mother slid open the glass door and ushered her children into the house. The 14-year-old girl said, "What were they doing, Mum?"

"Trespassing, Brooklyn," said the mother.

"I saw her boobs," said the boy.

"No, you didn't, Hugh Junior," said the mother.

Mitch lifted papers from the bag, and said, "Here it is. Is this 244 Bay Road?"

The mother looked accusingly at the father, who widened his eyes. Then she turned quickly and walked inside. The father paused and opened his mouth, then turned and followed his wife.

Mitch asked, "What's the address here?"

The door closed and they heard the clicking of a lock. Then they saw the parents inside, arguing.

Mitch and Annie dragged their suitcases to the least-exposed area of the deck, unzipped the bags, pulled out the first clothes they found, and dressed.

While they were still dressing, the sliding door opened just enough for the man's head to poke out. It swivelled left and right, looking for them. Then he noticed them near the bushes, and yelled, "There must be some mistake. We've already booked it."

Annie said, "How's that possible?"

"Don't know," said the man. "Better check with the owner."

Mitch pressed his phone, but nothing happened, and he said, "My phone doesn't work."

"No, it won't," said the man, "Australian SIM cards don't work here."

Mitch started to ask, "Can we just use—", but the man pulled his head in, closed the door, and locked it.

Mitch moved towards the glass door and said to Annie, "There must be some mistake. They'll help us."

Behind the glass, the whole family stood at the window, observing Annie and Mitch like exhibits in a zoo.

The two parties stared at each other through the glass for an extended period.

From inside the glass, the family saw Annie and Mitch talking to each other with exasperated looks on their faces.

"What are they saying?" said the boy.

"Nothing good," said the girl.

Then they saw Annie make the phone symbol with her thumb and pinkie pressed against her face, while mouthing the words, "Can we use your phone?"

The mother shook her head.

The daughter asked, "Why can't we let them use the phone, mummy?"

"They could be murderers," said the mother.

From outside, on the deck, Mitch and Annie saw the mother shake her head and mouth the word, "No." Then she pointed off the property and mimed, "Go!" in exaggeratedly wide words.

From inside the glass, the family watched Mitch open his mouth, then crunch his eyebrows together. Annie frowned, too. Then she pointed at the woman and exaggeratedly mimed the word, "Bitch."

From outside the glass, Mitch and Annie saw the boy put his hand to his mouth and giggle. His sister opened her mouth wide and smiled at her brother, then blanked her expression to look up at her mother.

The mother's eyes widened with outrage. Her shoulders swaggered, her head wobbled, and she pointed slowly at Annie and was about to say something, then looked down at her kids. She stopped, shielded her face so her kids wouldn't see, then mouthed the word, "Slut."

From inside the house, they saw Annie's eyes go wide and wild. Her jaw dropped with shock. Annie suddenly stepped up to the glass, and the whole family stepped back.

From outside the sliding door, Annie saw the family step back from the glass. Then the mother mimed the phone symbol and mouthed the word, "Police."

Annie threw her head back in exaggerated fake laughter, without any sound. Mitch glanced sideways at her.

Inside the glass, the family saw Annie slap her knee with hilarity. The mother tapped the glass, pointed to Annie and Mitch, and made the symbol for handcuffs. They saw Annie do another silent-movie laugh. Then she looked left and right, as if trying to find something, and disappeared from view. The family all stepped closer to the sliding door to look in the direction Annie had moved.

The four faces pressed against the glass and peered sideways to see where Annie had gone. Their heads jostled for position and their concerned eyes scanned to find the woman. Breath fogged the glass as they watched and waited, but they were quick to wipe away the mist so they could see where Annie had gone.

Suddenly, Annie jumped into view from the other direction, with her arms waving and her mouth wide in silent screaming. The family jumped back from the glass in shock. The man stumbled backwards over a lounge. The others family members restored him to his feet.

Recovering inside, the family saw Annie doubled over laughing and Mitch standing next to her appraising his wife with raised eyebrows. Annie held her chest, still heaving from the exertion of running around the house. Inside the house, the mother grabbed the phone from her husband and pressed buttons.

From outside on the deck, they saw the mother step closer to the glass, hold the phone to her ear, and stare intently at Annie.

From inside the glass, they saw Annie step closer to the glass and cross her arms and stare at the mother.

It was a Mexican stand-off. Two fierce warriors staring hatred at one another through the sliding glass door of a double-booked luxury Airbnb on a high cliff overlooking the two-blue view of the curvature of the earth.

One was holding a phone to her ear and tapping her foot. The other, outside, had her arms tightly crossed and her lips pursed into a sneer. They were so close their furious breaths faintly fogged the glass from both sides.

A few metres away, the cliff dropped away dramatically to relentless ocean waves smashing impenetrable basalt boulders.

Finally, Mitch put his arm around his wife's shoulders and eased her away from the glass. Annie's eyes were still fixed on the woman inside. Mitch steered her away and started gathering bags. With angry eyes, Annie looked towards him, then glanced back at the family. Then she lifted her head imperiously, turned on her heel, picked up a bag and walked haughtily in front of Mitch off the grounds of On Dar Cliff.

CHAPTER FIVE
POTHOLE

Our two Love Aliens trudged their three suitcases along the rough edge of a "quaint" country road for what seemed like ages.

Annie towed her extra-large, flowery suitcase behind her. Mitch towed Annie's matching, medium-sized, flowery case, and his own large Samsonite trundle, constantly fighting to keep the two suitcases from running into each other. He was wearing his neck brace again.

The wheels of all the cases clunked from one pothole into another.

After a particularly deep hole stopped him in his tracks, Mitch swore, "Fuck! You brought so many clothes!"

Annie stopped and said beguilingly, "To look beautiful for you, husband."

Mitch inhaled deeply, smiled, and said, "You look beautiful in nothing, wife."

"Young Hugh Junior certainly thought so," said Annie.

They laughed into an embrace and repeated sentences from their encounter with the family at the Airbnb.

"I saw her boobs," said Annie imitating the young boy's high-pitched voice.

"No, you didn't," said Mitch, quoting the mother and laughing.

Annie was laughing so much as she imitated the son, she had to gulp breaths between words, "What are ... they ... doing?"

Laughter made it impossible for either of them to complete the woman's response.

Mitch tried, "Trespa—" before laughter took over.

Annie said, "Trespass—" then doubled over.

Mitch inhaled deeply and said, "—passing," then leaned onto a suitcase, which fell over and caused them to laugh more.

When Annie could finally draw breath, she shook her head slightly and grinned mischievously, "We were so busted."

"Sooo busted," laughed Mitch, then turning serious said, "Can you believe they wouldn't let us use their phone?"

"Arseholes," said Annie.

"The Arsehole family."

"Mr and Mrs Arsehole. And the Arsehole children.

"Little Hugh Junior Arsehole and Brooklyn Arsehole."

"With names like that, what chance do they have?"

"Couldn't expect them to be anything else."

They laughed and hugged and kissed smoothly. They smiled into each other's eyes, then looked down at their luggage and along the potted country road rising into the green distance.

Annie stood straight and said, "Right-ho!"

Mitch, said, "Bags ... UP!" and they collected their respective handles.

Then they turned as one and started marching, towing their weaving, clunking luggage along the rough road.

About three metres later, "bang," Annie's flowery suitcase bumped into a particularly deep pothole and jolted from her hand and lost a wheel. Metal scraped harshly along the bitumen.

Annie swore and kicked her suitcase and said "Owh!"

She lifted her eyes from the offending bag and shook her head at Mitch. He smiled sympathetically. Annie sighed a sad smile.

"Together," she said.

"Together," he agreed.

"How's it even possible—the accommodation?"

"Double booked."

"Yes, Mitch, obviously," she retorted.

"Don't take it out on me, Annie, I didn't double book it."

"Didn't you, Mitch?! Didn't you book it?"

Mitch paused and said, "Yes, I did."

The fire in Annie's eyes suddenly cooled and she walked to Mitch, "Of course, you did, you lovely man."

He dropped the bags and they hugged in the middle of the country road, in the middle of green pastures, in the middle of Norfolk Island, in the middle of the Pacific Ocean.

Then they felt the first drops of rain.

Annie sneezed. They looked around and saw fat white cows, tan cows, grey cows, they saw cute chocolate calves and lots of lush green paddocks, but nowhere to shelter.

"At least it'll wash off the last of the blood," said Annie, and they start laughing again.

"And the shit," laughed Mitch.

Through fatigue, hunger, and absurdity, the laughter rose a notch, becoming slightly hysterical.

Doubled over and fighting for breath, Mitch said, "And tiny remnants of vomit."

Annie weakly approached him and touched his ear, "Any chunks of carrot behind your ears."

They fell into each other with tears and rain streaming down their faces, sharing their Love Alien humour that was so good it was almost worth the pain and shame and gross embarrassment of the last four hours.

Annie lifted her face to the sky, closed her eyes and smiled up at the clouds while rain washed her face. Mitch marvelled at her beauty in that perfect moment, and a smile spread across his face.

Annie opened an eye on him, and Mitch beamed even more broadly. He leant his head back to feel the rain fall on his face, then spread his arms wide and yelled, "Yahooo!"

Annie opened her arms and yelled, more emphatically, "Yahooooo!" to the rain and the clouds and the sky.

Mitch went to her, lifting and spinning her in his arms right there in the middle of the country road. The rain fell harder, and they kissed. They picked up their suitcases and carried them over their heads as cover from the downpour.

Mitch tried to balance the two cases but after toppling both, he lay his Samsonite trundle beside the road and un-zipped it.

"I'll leave it here," said Mitch. "No one will nick it. Or if they do—" pulling out a pair of underpants, "—good luck to them."

He dug through the clothes for a shirt and some pants. Annie leaned in and lifted up a fine dark suit, and said, "Wow, you were dressing to impress."

"I thought we might have a candle-lit dinner one night," he laughed, "under the stars."

"That's quite likely," she said, "because it looks like we'll be sleeping under the stars."

Annie folded his jacket carefully, tucking it under her arm while she unzipped one of her flowery suitcases. Clothes blossomed into the dirt. She removed a dress and two pairs of shoes and replaced them with Mitch's suit jacket and a loud red Hawaiian shirt that she'd plucked from his bag, saying "You'll need a shirt to go with that suit."

They swapped a few more pieces between suitcases, then Mitch slid his case under a roadside bush.

In the middle of the road, Annie sat on her suitcase, and took the opportunity to steal a kiss from Mitch as he zipped it shut – their consolidation complete.

CHAPTER SIX

SULLEN

Sometimes, an unlucky cloud gets snagged on Norfolk Island – the only chunk of land in hundreds of kilometres of ocean.

The cloud would be whistling along, enjoying the scenery. Maybe watching its own reflection glide along the shining surface of the Pacific Ocean. Relishing the thrill of flying low, going with the flow, then suddenly it'd notice the little island ahead. The rough volcanic upthrust coming fast. And it'd be like, "Whoa! Whoa!" But too late. Unable to steer around the 318-metre peak of Mount Pitt in time, it rips its underbelly on the peak. Then, like a bladder bag's been ripped open, the cloud empties its entire payload in a deluge in one spot on Norfolk Island.

On this day, that spot is halfway between Captain Cook Lookout and Burnt Pine township. Directly over Annie and Mitch, trudging along Anson Bay Road.

Annie sneezed.

They were almost impossible to see through the curtain of rain as they bumbled along the muddy edge of the potholed bitumen. By squinting, you could just make out the figure of Annie carrying her flowered suitcase over her head. The hard-shell suitcase was acting like a restrictor valve on a modern shower head; it limited the volume of water showering onto Annie; until she sneezed – which she did every ten metres or so – moving the suitcase and exposing her to a full gush of 1970s showerhead splurge.

Mitch was a few steps in front, hunched forwards at the waist, carrying Annie's extra-large suitcase along his back like a very lost, very drenched, very tall, Himalayan sherpa.

Both their heads were downcast, and their eyes were squinted tight against the spray, so they could see their next step. But even if they were wide-eyed and looking ahead, they couldn't see far through the sheet of rain.

The same could be said for 86-year-old, Mary Christian-Bailey, who at that moment was driving her Daihatsu van between Captain Cook Lookout and Burnt Pine township, along Anson Bay Road.

Even though she was hunched over the wheel and squinting through her spectacles to see through the full-speed wipers, she could barely make out the patch of potholed bitumen directly in front of her car.

Mary's concentration wasn't helped by an awful country-disco remix of Creedence Clearwater Revival's "Bad Moon Rising" playing loudly on the radio, courtesy of Norfolk's own radio station.

The ghostly shapes of the two travellers suddenly appeared from the torrent. Mary reflexively swerved the van – whose skinny tyres weren't very good at swerving even in dry conditions – and the van skidded instead. Then it jolted through a series of potholes, shaking Mary like a saltshaker, before bumping into the ditch on the wrong side of the road.

Mitch looked up from under the suitcase and said, "Oh, fuck. What now?"

Annie sneezed, "Just go see who we've killed this time."

Mitch lowered the flowery suitcase into a puddle and limped across to the car, tugging absent-mindedly at his saturated neck brace.

The first thing Mitch noticed when he opened the passenger door was the warmth of the cabin. The second thing was the warmth of Mary's smile shining at him. The third thing was the awful cover of "Bad Moon Rising" on the radio.

"I think the potholes saved me," Mary said. "Slowed me down. Remind me to write a letter to the council thanking them." She erupted into a laugh that warmed Mitch's heart like sitting in front of a log fire. He wanted to make her laugh again just for the warmth of it, but all he could say was, "Warm."

"You're not walking in this, are you?" said Mary.

"Well, sort of," said Mitch, "Slowly. Very slowly."

"Get in," said Mary.

By now Annie had arrived, and she leaned into the cabin and asked, "You're not hurt?!"

"No," said Mary, "I'm fine."

"After the day we've had," Annie sneezed, "I'd have bet we'd killed you."

"Jump in and tell me about it," said Mary.

But first, Mitch and Annie had to push the little van backwards out of the ditch and throw their cases in the tray back. Then they jumped in and started regaling Mary with their Airbnb story. But they gradually fell silent, watching

Mary steer a terrifying 14-point turn – forward and back-wards – across the narrow and nearly invisible road. Until, by extraordinary good fortune, the small van hadn't been T-boned by an oncoming car and was safely facing the way it'd come.

"Double booked, you say?" asked Mary.

"Eh?" said Mitch.

"Your accommodation," said Mary.

"Double booked, yes," said Annie.

"Yes, of course, it's the silly season," said Mary. "They do that. But some people are just scurrilous, aren't they."

"Yes," agreed Annie.

"Scurrilous," agreed Mitch.

"Whose place was it?"

"244 Bay Road," said Mitch.

"Oh, no, I don't know street numbers," said Mary. "Near Tom and Laura's old place—no, of course you won't know them, will you?"

"No," said Annie.

"Of course, silly me," said Mary. "Is it before or after the bend?"

"Ahhh—past some cows," said Annie.

"After the winery?" Asked Mary.

"Ahhh—on a cliff," ventured Mitch.

"On Dar Cliff?" asked Mary.

"On Dar Cliff!" said Mitch excitedly.

"Oh, yes. Buck's old place," said Mary, "The new own-ers are from away."

Mary lowered her voice as if telling a secret – just in case someone in the glovebox was listening to their conversation, "They've never come here apart from the once, I think."

"Scurrilous," said Annie.

"Scurrilous," said Mary and they laughed. Then Mary said, "Now, of course, there'll be nowhere else to stay."

"What?" chorused Annie and Mitch.

"Gosh, no!" said Mary, "Silly season." Which apparently explained everything from transport to housing. Possibly even their entire honeymoon. The newlyweds looked desperately at each other.

"Oh well, looks like you're staying at mine tonight," said Mary. "Then I can ring around to see who else has somewhere they're not using."

"Oh, no," said Mitch half-heartedly, but Annie squeezed his thigh.

"Thank you so much," said Annie.

But Mary hadn't heard either of them. Her words continued to relay exactly what she was thinking, "I think Tilly and Link – the Abbot girl – are away in Brisbane." Then dropping her voice again into a whisper, "She's getting her boobs done, but they're telling everyone it's her sinuses again," then looking back at the road, "so I'll ask Len tomorrow."

Mary squinted at her watch, while her passengers glared, terrified, at the barely visible road ahead.

Mary said, "Too late, now, though. He'll be at the Bowl-o. And we're home soon."

"Are you sure it's no bother?" asked Annie.

"No bother at all," said Mary. "A lovely young couple to keep me company. Plus, my Bernie would never have allowed visitors to the island to be shipwrecked without a place to stay. No one would've in the old days. I don't know what's happened to the place sometimes."

"Scurrilous," said Mitch.

"Scurrilous," laughed Mary. And the warmth of it permeated their wet clothes.

"Where's your car?" asked Mary.

"We had ah-ah-an accident," stuttered Annie.

"Oh, no, you poor things," said Mary. "Just tell me it isn't your honeymoon."

They were silent.

Mary looked at them and laughed, "It is!"

She took both hands off the wheel, and clapped, "Oh, priceless!" Then she laughed that same crackling fireplace laugh that warmed our lovers' hearts and restored their faith in the world of humans.

They didn't quite raise their cold hands to warm them in the old lady's giggling glow, but they did share a look that said, in their Love Alien language, "This planet *is* fit for habitation."

Smiles resurfaced on their cheeks, and they talked and jostled together on that cramped bench seat as Mary drove them into every pothole on the way to her house.

Eventually they turned off the road through a gap in the high hedges. The rain stopped suddenly as they drove under a canopy of tall tree ferns along a dark avenue carved through rainforest.

Mary pointed to the tall ferns, "See these tree ferns?"

"Yes," they chorused.

"Tallest tree ferns in the world," said Mary. "Endemic to Norfolk Island."

"Really," said Annie, and they looked with renewed admiration at the tall rainforest tree ferns.

"Ha, there's the teacher in me coming out," Mary laughed. "Class over."

"It's a unique island," said Mitch.

"Unique for ruining my honeymoon," murmured Annie.

Mary laughed, "You've had a rough trot, but the island'll sort you out." Then looking up to the trees she whispered, "She loves love."

Raising their eyebrows to one another, the lovers shared a glance of concern then looked ahead through the archway of trees into a bright clearing of lush gardens, a large pond, and a huge lawn with football goal posts at the far end.

Running alongside the lawn was a long two-storey timber house with gables and a wide veranda.

The cloud had apparently emptied its bag and moved on. Now sunlight sparkled across the big lawn which shone with a bright lime aura, as if the saturation had been turned up in Photoshop. The corrugated roof glinted silver, and the white trims of the windows blinked like they were just waking up.

There were ducks waddling around the pond and three large white geese goose-stepping from a large coop. Then came a rooster and some hens towing a single file of fluffy chicks. Finally, a peacock emerged, immediately fanning its feathers like he was opening his eyes to see who'd arrived.

The geese barked at the new arrivals.

"Settle down, Remy," said Mary to the excited pup. "These are my new friends." Then turning to Annie and Mitch with amused shock, "I don't even know your names!"

They introduced themselves then Mary introduced them to Gilbert the Goose, Liberace the Peacock, and Mick Jagger, the rooster.

"I won't introduce you to the chickens yet," said Mary, "but I'm Mary Christian-Bailey."

They all shook hands and Mary shuffled towards the house, saying, "You look like you could do with a tub. I'll put a fire on and see what we can rummage up for dinner."

Mitch and Annie followed her like the chicks following their hen.

CHAPTER SEVEN

BUNGALOW

Built in 1890 by a descendant of Fletcher Christian, Mary's house is a South Pacific version of a Californian bungalow, with wide verandahs and big bay windows offering an eyeful of wide blue ocean. But before you get to that, it's the timber construction that draws your eye – to boards that are three-times wider and longer than you'd expect.

Mitch tapped them as he entered, saying "Solid," more to himself than anyone else.

Then he said, "Reminds you that this little island is home to some very big trees, the Norfolk Island Pines."

"And people who know how to use them," said Mary.

The walls inside were lined with framed photographs showing large gatherings of Norfolk families in front of this house. Some photos were black and white, some sepia, some 70s Kodachrome, and some digital printouts. All had four or five generations represented.

"The house has been extended by succeeding generations," said Mary as she led Annie and Mitch through bright rooms trapped in time, "The New Zealand army even requisitioned it during World War Two."

Above the fireplace, a royal portrait shared prime position with a kid's drawing of *Sonic the Hedgehog*.

"My grandson's mad about Sonic," said Mary, then pointing to a painting of an ancestral home in England, she said, "that's Fletcher Christian's childhood home in Cumberland."

Annie and Mitch were suitably impressed and harmonised an "Ooh" sound, stretched across three tones. Anywhere else it might've been mistaken for a bird call, but here it's understood as a polite alternative to a repeated "Wow".

Leaning against the wall, next to the blackened fireplace, was a long-handled brass pan with an engraved lid.

"What's that?" asked Mitch.

"A bed warmer," said Mary. "You put coals in it, then slide it between the sheets an hour or so before you go to bed. We actually got it on our honeymoon."

"No!" said Annie.

"Yes," Mary laughed, "I don't know why we got it. We were in Europe. We saw it and perhaps both of us appreciated history, or antiques. We didn't know each other well."

"What do you mean?" asked Mitch.

Mary explained: "Bernie was from here, and I was visiting Norfolk Island with my father. A holiday, of sorts. I met Bernie while I was here. And—well it's amazing really."

Mary turned to face them, and smiled, "On my last night here, Bernie asked me to go out. And at the end of that night, he asked me to marry him."

Mary paused to appreciate the looks on her guests' faces, then she continued, "And I said 'yes'."

"No!" said Annie.

"Yes," giggled Mary.

"After only knowing each other a few days?" said Mitch.

"I was going home the next day," said Mary. "He had to make his move then and there."

"Scurrilous," said Annie.

"Totally," said Mary. "So, we didn't know each other well, but we found out about each other a bit on the honeymoon."

Annie and Mitch smiled at each other.

"But don't worry too much about the honeymoon. It's nothing. We had lots of them, actually."

Annie asked, "How long were you married?"

Mary said, "Fifty-five years."

"No!" said Annie.

"Yes!" laughed Mary.

"And your secret?" asked Annie.

Mary shook her head and said, "Everyone has to make their own path." Then she paused and added, "But I'd say, commitment. We weren't really in love when we met. But we committed to each other, and the love grew."

Then she walked on. The lovers found each other's hands and followed.

They walked past poured-glass windows that looked out to rainforest groves and ocean glimpses. Mary noticed a spider in the corner, and said, "I'll open the window and see if she wants to go out."

She did and the three of them watched the spider leave. Then they walked along a thin corridor lined with bookshelves containing cookbooks, kids' books, gardening books, history tomes, the complete set of *Encyclopedia*

Britannica from 1989, reams of music scores, and the complete set of Dickens which Mary said was a wedding present in 1967.

They continued the tour up a set of stairs built from newer timber, to a cosy loft at the apex of several different roofs from various extensions over the nineteenth, twentieth and twenty-first centuries.

On one wall, a timber frame was divided into ten smaller frames, each containing a sewing bobbin.

"I keep them because they won't be around in future," said Mary, "so I rescue them."

"You're a historian," said Mitch.

"I rescue things," she said.

"And people," said Annie.

Mary laughed and pointed to a pile of blankets, "I also rescue old blankets for those people to keep warm."

"And we're very glad you do," said Mitch wrapping one around his wife's shoulders and one around himself.

"Restore rather than replace," Mary said. "Part of the resourceful nature of Norfolk Islanders."

CHAPTER EIGHT

WIFE

After Annie and Mitch had showered, and dressed in their driest clothes, they went down to the kitchen and sat at the table in front of Mary's old wood-fired Aga stove.

Mitch noted that it was even warmer in there than Mary's laugh. Annie noted that her blocked nose meant she'd lost her sense of smell. Which was a shame because the warm kitchen wafted the aroma of rich lamb stew, that Mary said would, "warm their bones."

She served it up and said grace. They savoured their first meal since losing their lunch on the plane.

"Definitely the best meal I've ever had," said Mitch.

Annie nodded and sneezed.

Mary laughed, "Save room for golden syrup pudding."

Mitch rubbed his stomach and moaned. Annie sneezed her hair forwards into the stew.

After dessert, the newlyweds were radiating with the warmth of full bellies and human kindness as they floated upstairs to their bedroom.

Their small double bed was layered with cotton sheets, feather eiderdowns and knitted blankets. The two weary newlyweds slipped into it, like a penis into a vagina, and "Oooh"-ed and "Ahhh"-ed accordingly.

Then Annie sneezed.

And again.

And again.

Then Mitch got up to get a glass of water for his wife. He slipped back into bed again.

Then he slid out. This time for her toiletries bag with the herbal echinacea.

Then he slipped in again.

Then he slid out. This time for *his* toiletries bag and his antihistamines.

Then he slipped in again.

And finally, when Annie was calm and blowing her red runny nose, and Mitch was in bed looking at Annie blowing her red runny nose, they agreed by non-verbal cues that this was as close to a penis in a vagina they'd get.

Much sneezing and coughing later, any chances of sleep seemed beaten. But at 2:30 am Mitch finally fell asleep, with Annie propped up beside him on luscious pillows, sniffling, coughing, and watching her husband of 31 long hours, snoring quietly.

Her blue eyes were puffy and tinged with red, but they softened while gazing at his beautiful face. So peaceful. Then she sneezed. She quickly looked back at him and was glad she hadn't woken him. But perversely, she was also disappointed that Mitch hadn't automatically been woken by the signal of his new wife's distress.

Annie waited for the next sneeze with scientific curiosity, just like she would've in the primary industries lab in Brisbane where she worked as a biologist. She waited and observed because: a) she was a scientist trained to experiment; b) she had nothing better to do; and c) she was sick and tired and dismally pissed-off.

When the sneeze racked her frame, she immediately recovered and observed her subject: *Subject paused snoring for two seconds, then resumed.*

Annie was tempted to take notes but lacking resources, merely drummed her fingers on the blanket, cocked an eyebrow, and waited patiently for the next sneeze.

This time she was careful not to muffle the explosion with hanky or palm. She just let it rip for the maximum effect of sound echoing off walls in their small room. Then she observed: *No response. Hardly discernible disruption to breathing pattern.*

"No response!" she said loudly, "I could be dying here!" Which, she also noted caused no interruption to the blissful sleeping of her partner who, not even two days earlier, had devotedly pledged "... in sickness and in health".

The wife–scientist intensified the experiment immediately. Instead of waiting for the next sneeze, Annie coughed loudly and used the sound to cover hitting the subject on the forehead. Mitch immediately sat upright in bed and turned to his new wife, who was now dead still with eyes closed, pretending sleep.

Mitch looked up at the ceiling and around the room, holding his forehead and frowning in confusion. Then he slowly lay back down and closed his eyes.

Still with her eyes closed, Annie asked, "Aren't you even going to ask if I'm OK?"

"Are you OK?" asked Mitch groggily.

"Well, now that you ask, no," said Annie, sitting haughtily against the pillows, arms folded and red-tinged eyes now wide open, leering down at Mitch. She looked like a slightly unhinged monarch.

"Now that you ask," she said, "I'm truly worried about what other pledges of our marriage contract you didn't take seriously."

"What?" asked Mitch.

"Faithfulness? Hmmm?" she asked, "Did you think it'd be OK to root around?"

"What?" asked Mitch.

"Richer or poorer?" asked Annie. "Things get rough, you gonna hit the road? Are you? Hmmm?"

"What?" asked Mitch frowning. Then it dawned on him, "Oh, wait—is this because you're sick? Was I sleeping?"

Astounded to have been caught out so quickly by a man so recently in REM sleep, all the queen could do was turn regally away.

"Oh, baby, I'm sorry," said Mitch, "I didn't mean to fall asleep. I wish I had the cold instead of you. Here—" he said moving his face closer to hers, "give it to me."

"Stop it," said Annie.

"No, I want it," Mitch said. "I'll take it off you."

Smiling despite herself, Annie said, "Stop it, you fool. OK, OK."

"We share everything," he said.

They giggled and wriggled and snuggled. And both woke with full-blown colds.

CHAPTER NINE

VICTORIA'S EXPERIMENT

It was their second morning waking up in a bed together as a married couple. They smiled at each other in the bathroom mirror while cleaning their teeth. They smiled as they nudged past each other while trying to find dry clothes.

They said, "Excuse me," and, "I love you," and, "Can you see my socks?"

They joined forces to figure out the order of command for the layers of bed linen while making the bed. And they sniffled around the attic in their shared Love-Alien glow.

Annie was the first to notice the brilliant blue sea when she was brushing her hair near the attic window. She pointed out the window and said, "Wow, look at this, Mitch."

Mitch did, and his eyes widened at the breathtaking expanse of Pacific Ocean.

He opened the window to better comprehend the enormity of the glistening blue sea between them and the horizon. They poked their heads out the window and looked all the way to the right, where the sea disappeared behind a clump of ancient trees in Mary's garden. Then their two pairs of eyes crawled back along the bulging blue curve of horizon, all the way to the opposite point of the compass, where the shore rose in a jagged graph-line of Norfolk pine silhouettes.

The ocean filled their view and made their chests expand. It felt like their hearts were yearning to fly through the air and dive into that blue. A few fluffy clouds were migrating along the horizon from somewhere in the west to somewhere in the east.

Annie hugged Mitch and their hearts beat against each other as they shared the view. Then Mitch sneezed and grimaced in pain, touching his neck. Annie cooed sympathetically, then coughed. They sniffled and smiled sadly and helped each other downstairs to the kitchen where Mary was cooking.

"Hello, love birds," said Mary.

"Herro," said Annie and Mitch.

"Oh no, you got yourselves a sniffle?" said Mary. "I'm not surprised, the way you two were galivanting around in the rain yesterday."

They laughed and sneezed.

"You sit yourselves down, here, near the stove. We've got an omelette. The girls delivered a baker's dozen for you this morning."

"The girls?" asked Mitch.

"The hens, dearest," said Mary. "The chooks. Usually, I can't coax half of them to lay, but they must've decided you needed some Norfolk hospitality."

Mary served bright yellow omelettes onto Spode dinner plates with blue-and-white farmyard scenes.

"Hospitality used to be very important on Norfolk Island. We used to be like one big family." Mary pointed to an intricate flax weaving hanging from the wall, "See that? The girls gave it to me as a tribute at Bernie's funeral, last year."

"The girls?" asked Mitch.

Mary laughed, "Ha, no, not the chooks. Although some of them fuss like old hens. No, this was from my girlfriends. It's an old Pitcairn custom to make a weaving as a tribute."

Mary carefully folded her tea-towel on the table in front of her, and said without looking up, "Not that young'uns would be interested in all that old history, now."

Annie said, "We'd love to know."

So, as they ate, they were treated to a history of Norfolk Island from an esteemed elder and keeper of tales. It went something like this:

"Norfolk Island is the highest point on an underwater mountain range, known as the Norfolk Ridge, which runs all the way from New Zealand up to New Caledonia. The only place this 1200-kilometre range rises above sea level is for the 8 kilometres of Norfolk Island and tiny Phillip Island just to its south.

"Captain Cook claimed the island for England in 1774, thinking that the tall, straight Norfolk Island Pines would make good masts for the Empire's expanding naval fleet, and the flax would make great canvas for sails. The British settled the island in 1788 to harvest and export, but the timber and flax weren't as helpful as they'd hoped so they shut the settlement down after 26 years.

"Then in 1825, the British government devised a better use for Norfolk Island," said Mary. "They reopened the colony as a penal settlement for the worst convicts in the Empire. And Her Majesty's courts supplied repeat offenders to build it."

"Many of those convicts were bound for the gallows," said Mary, "but were given a choice: death by hanging or a life sentence on Norfolk Island. Hard to know which hell would've been worse, but many gave it a go. They sent 30,000 convicts here over the next 70 years."

"Where was the colony?" asked Mitch.

"Oh, the old buildings are still down at Kingston," said Mary.

"We haven't seen any of this yet," said Annie.

"It's breath-taking to see the big old gaol so close to that perfect beach," said Mary.

"Like they were teasing the convicts," said Mitch.

"Adding insult to injury," said Mitch.

"Meanwhile, in another part of the Pacific, near Tonga," said the retired teacher, "Lieutenant Fletcher Christian led a violent mutiny against Captain Bligh aboard HMS *Bounty*."

"The famous *Mutiny on the Bounty*," said Annie, "I've seen the film."

"The one with Marlon or Mel?"

"Mel Gibson."

"I saw the one with Brando," said Mitch.

"That one's my favourite," said Mary, "Trevor Howard was so ruthless as Bligh."

"I think it was Anthony Hopkins as Bligh in the one I saw," said Annie.

"So good," said Mary, "Well you'll know the mutineers forced Bligh and eighteen of crew into a small boat with enough supplies to get them over the horizon. Then the mutineers sailed off for a four-month tiki tour of the Pacific, especially Tahiti, where they managed to kidnap fourteen Polynesian women and six Polynesian men."

Mary unfolded a large map on the kitchen table so Annie and Mitch could follow the lesson. Then the retired teacher pointed with a wooden spoon to a small dot in the middle of the South Pacific Ocean, and said, "See Pitcairn Island? Way out here, in the middle of nowhere."

Mitch and Annie leant in close to the map to see the tiny brown dot in the blue sea.

"Very small," said Annie.

"And rugged," said Mary, "But it had two advantages.'

Mary counted on her fingers: "One, it was able to sustain life. And two, it was wrongly recorded on the British maps."

"Really," said Mitch.

"Yes," said Mary, "They'd mapped it about two hundred nautical miles away from its actual position."

"So," Mary asked her pupils, "why do you think that was an advantage?"

Annie and Mitch studied each other to see if the answer was written on their faces. And it turned out, by facial expression, eyebrow twisting, and lip pursing, the Love Aliens were able to figure it out.

Annie said, "Because it wasn't where the British thought."

Mitch said, "And they were looking for the mutineers."

Annie said, "So the British ships couldn't find them?"

"Well done," said Mary the teacher. "The British didn't find those mutineers on Pitcairn, so they didn't get killed by a British hangman. Instead, they were killed by each other on that little dot. And by the Tahitian blokes they'd taken as slaves. And sometimes even by their women.

"But those Tahitian women also had time to grow food and make clothes and raise the children. So, the colony thrived on that rough little island."

"Amazing," said Annie.

"The last mutineer, Adams, taught them all to read from the Bible and ran the colony under Christian principles," said Mary, "And Queen Victoria eventually got wind of this remote Christian outpost in the Pacific."

"How did she find out about it?" asked Mitch.

"The Pitcairners sent a letter to Britain asking for leniency," said Mary, "And as luck would have it, Queen Victoria was closing down her penal colony on Norfolk Island and was in the mood for a social experiment."

"How many people were there on Pitcairn by then," asked Mitch.

"There were 193 people living on little Pitcairn Island by 1856. All descended from the eight mutineers and their Tahitian hostages. And all of them were transported from Pitcairn Island to Norfolk Island, for Victoria's Experiment, with the addition of a baby born en route."

"Amazing," said Annie.

"Isn't it," said Mary. And continued, "They settled into the houses and buildings of the former penal colony. It was the first time these Pitcairn Islanders had ever cooked inside.

" 'The experiment' as it was called, was like a Victorian, *Big Brother* without the cameras. Each of the extended families of the eight mutineers were allocated 50 acres. Isolated from all outside influences, it was hoped great things would grow from a community built on Christian principles and temperance."

"They survived and thrived," said Mitch, who was now washing the breakfast plates.

"Victoria's experiment worked," said Annie who was drying.

"Well," said Mary, "the temperance didn't last long but the Christianity did. And for 150 years it's been a thriving success."

"Everything grew in the volcanic soil. The ocean was jumping with fish and there were cattle left over from the colony. They were self-sufficient for 80 years.

"Then, in World War Two, the Americans wanted Norfolk Island because of its strategic position in the Pacific. They helped the Australian and the New Zealand armies build an airbase and runway."

"That would've changed things for the island, wouldn't it?" asked Mitch.

"Oh, yes, the runway changed everything. Many planes staged through here during the war. Then afterwards, tourists could fly in," said Mary smiling, "Norfolk became a pretty wild place for a while. Even became a tax haven in 1966, which lured a lot of wealthy people to the island, like Colleen McCollough and Helen Reddy. Then in 2016, Australia called in its markers and took over control."

"Now it's an Australian external territory," said Mary, "Which is either good for business or bad for democracy, depending on which side of the fence you're sitting. Me, I think it's good to have healthcare, but we do need an elected voice in government."

Then Mary started counting on her fingers again: "One, our electorate is in the Australian Capital Territory. Two, our postcode is in New South Wales. Three, our health and education are run by Queensland. And four, our phone code is the same as the Antarctic, which is six thousand kilometres away."

Annie and Mitch both shook their heads slowly.

Mitch finally said, "You're kidding?"

"Nope. All true. Australia wouldn't want to cede its independence because of Norfolk Island's strategic location. I heard someone describe it once as a stationary aircraft carrier in the Pacific, about 800 kilometres from the nearest land."

Annie said, "Especially with all eyes looking towards the Pacific at the moment."

"Yes," said Mary, "So it's nice we speak similar languages, but we need to elect our own government so we can voice our needs about local issues."

By now all three were sipping tea.

"Ahhh, there you go," said Mary. "Lecture over."

"It's amazing," said Mitch, "I never knew any of that."

"Sorry to prattle on, I just love history," said Mary.

"No, it's fascinating," said Annie.

"Hard to believe such a little place can fit so much in," said Mitch.

"Yes," said Mary. "Speaking of fitting things in, I called around my network and there's no accommodation at all."

Mitch said, "Silly season."

"Fast learner," said Mary. "Everyone's got family visiting for Christmas."

Annie and Mitch looked at each other.

"But you're welcome to stay here with me," said Mary.

"Oh, that's lovely," said Annie, "but we couldn't."

"Nonsense," said Mary, "I like the company—and having someone to listen to me talk about my favourite subject, Norfolk Island, takes me back to my teaching days."

Just then a male voice sang out from the front of the house, "Mu-um."

"In here, George," said Mary.

Then turning to Annie and Mitch, she said, "This is my youngest."

In walked a solid dark-haired man about 40 years old wearing a flannelette shirt, faded shorts and woolly socks on his feet.

He saw the couple: "What the hell are you doing here?!"

"George!" said Mary.

The man stepped in front of his mother, "What are you doing to my mum?"

"Having breakfast," said Mitch.

"George!" said Mary, "This lovely couple—"

"Ran over Mildred," said George.

"What?" said Mary.

"Yesterday," said George. "Didn't they tell you?"

Mary and George looked at the offenders.

Annie said, "We didn't think it was—"

George said, "Important?"

"Appropriate," said Annie, "to tell a lovely lady about a tragedy we'd been involved in."

"It was a terrible accident," said Mitch to Mary. Then turning to George, "How did you know?"

"It's our cow!" said George.

"Oh no!" cried Mary. George held his mother.

Annie squinted at George and said, "You're related to the—"

"Related?" arced George. "I'm related to it alright. I own it."

"No, not the cow," said Annie, "The two women."

"Oh yes," said George, "Smiley and Polly."

"Oh no," said Mitch, Annie and Mary.

"We didn't know it was your cow, Mary," said Annie.

"Or that this was your mum, George," said Mitch.

"Oh, poor Mildred," said Mary, and started to cry.

"We're so sorry," said Annie, and started to cry.

"You will be when you get the bill," said George.

"Oh," said Mitch taken back. "Umh, how much do you think that will be?"

George started counting on his fingers, "Well there's loss of meat—loss of a beloved pet—loss of future income—"

"Is she dead?" asked Annie.

"Not yet," said George, "but her leg's bad. We'll know in a day or two if we have to put her down. Then look out!"

"George," said Mary, "don't be malicious."

George said, "Ten dollars a kilo. And she was at least three hundred kilos—"

Mitch, incredulous, "Three thousand dollars?"

Annie stopped crying and looked at Mitch, shocked.

"What are you doing here anyway?" asked George of the newlyweds.

"Staying the night," said Mitch.

"Our Airbnb was double-booked, and we were walking—and your mum—" said Annie, and started crying again.

Mary started crying again, too. The two women consoled each other.

"Well good!" said George. "You'd *better* stay here. So we can make sure you don't run off without paying."

That stopped everyone crying.

Mary: "George!"

George: "Sorry Mum, but it'll be considerable."

Annie said to Mitch, "Will our insurance cover it?"

George: "Typical."

Mary: "George!"

Mitch asked George, "What does that mean?"

Annie: "Mitch!"

George told Mitch, "It means you better not leave town, Bub."

Mitch asked George, "Bub?"

Annie said, "Mitch!"

George told Mitch, "That's right. Bub."

Mary said "George!"

Mitch told George, "Listen, Bub—"

Annie: "Mitch!"

George asked Mitch, "Oh, Bub, is it?"

Mary: "George!"

Mitch told George, "Yeah. Bub!"

George poked his finger into Mitch's chest, "No, you're Bub."

Annie: "Mitch!"

Mitch poked George and said, "Bub bub bub bub bu—"

Mary interjected, "Boobies!"

They all looked at her.

Mary continued, "George, you're acting like a masked booby."

Mitch and Annie looked at George, bewildered.

George turned and explained, "It's a bird."

"Yes," said Mary. "A very spoilt, baby bird that turns mean when it doesn't get its way. And you're acting like one, George."

Then she waved her hand towards Annie and Mitch and said, "Annie and Bub had a terrible accident."

Mitch said, "Mitch."

Mary asked, "What did I say?"

"Bub," said Mitch.

Mary giggled and said, "Sorry. Annie and Mitch had a terrible accident. They're a lovely young couple. And they're my guests! Your father would turn in his grave if he heard you acting like that to visitors. They're welcome to stay—or go, as they please. They're *my* guests. And you'll stop acting like an aatuti."

Annie and Mitch looked at George to translate, who said, "It's a fish."

"Yes," said Mary, "a very angry little fish."

And George hung his head, just slightly.

"Now if you all don't mind," said Mary, "I'd like a bit of time to myself to pray for poor Mildred."

"The cow," said George.

"Yes George," said Mary, "Thank you, the cow. Now, may I suggest you put your tour-guiding skills to good use and take our visitors to the bay for a snorkel."

Immediate grunts of disapproval from all, except Mary who said, "You swim don't you?"

Annie and Mitch said, "Yes."

"Good," said Mary, "there's gear in the garage. George will show you. See you all for lunch."

Like three chastened schoolkids, they shuffled out with their heads lowered. But Annie turned sadly from the doorway to say, "I'm so sorry about Mildred."

"Me, too, love," said Mary. "I pray she'll be ok."

CHAPTER TEN

BAY

George packed snorkels, masks and flippers into the back of his small ute, then tapped the metal tray back and whistled. A burly red cattle dog raced from under the shade of nearby trees and hurtled onto the tray. George leashed the dog to the back of the cabin so he wouldn't fall out on sharp corners, then said, "Meet Blue."

Annie and Mitch said, "Hi Blue."

Blue didn't say anything. He just perched his front legs on the side of the tray and leaned out as far as his tether would allow, so he could feel the wind on his furry face during the drive.

Inside the cabin of the ute, the three uncomfortable companions sat bunched together on the small bench seat. Their elbows nudged each other's ribs with every corner as they bumped along the country road from one pothole to the next.

The thin road ahead was hemmed on either side with dark-green forests of mature Norfolk pine tree waving their limbs in the breeze. The younger pines are a more brilliant lime green and have branches tilted more upwards, giving them a slightly startled look, like they're surprised to be here. And if trees could see, these ones would probably be surprised to see the three adult humans in the small ute leaning hard into each other with each corner in the road.

Around one particularly painful corner, the forests gave way to verdant pastures dotted with cows. George's little ute cruised over a rise, and the panorama opened to one of the most spectacular ocean views the two tourists had ever seen. They all stopped niggling and stared.

One hundred and eighty degrees of turquoise ocean all the way to the horizon, with only two small islands for relief. In the foreground, the green tabletop of tiny Nepean Island. And further south, Phillip Island, which looked like a misplaced chunk of the Australian outback had been airlifted from the Red Centre and plopped, right there, into the blue Pacific Ocean between Norfolk Island and the horizon.

George stopped the ute at Queen Elizabeth Lookout. Annie and Mitch fell out of the car, led by their wide eyes. Their hands found each other's again as they stared at the twinkling sea.

They looked first to the undulating ocean swells growing towards shore where they smashed on the coral reef of Emily Bay. The whole, wild, wet world dissipated over the reef and hissed into calm in that perfect bay.

They could see a coral reef enclosing a lagoon, about 100 metres from a white sandy beach. It separated the Pacific Ocean from the local swimming bay: the wild from the tame, the chaos from the calm, and the rest of the world from Norfolk Island. They'd read that this thin line of reef protects perfect Emily Bay from big waves, strong currents, and sharks. Making it arguably the world's best swimming pool.

From the lookout, Annie and Mitch could see a forest of startled pines next to the manicured greens of the golf course. And next to the greens were more blues, in the glassy waters of Cemetery Bay. Their eyes rested on the bommies of coral colour protected from ocean waves by another wide reef.

The contrast to Emily Bay was startling: a broken shore of jagged coral stone smoothed into bright white sandy beach, fringed by long pale marram grass that transformed into the trimmed pristine lawns of the island's cemetery with rows of freshly tended gravestones dating from the earliest days of the penal colony, in the late 1700s, up to the marker for Fudgie's funeral last week.

Looking closer, their eyes follow a row of picturesque historical houses – Quality Row – built in the 1830s for the officers of the penal colony.

From their viewpoint at the lookout, 170 metres above the fairways of the golf course, the rows of pines looked like Lego trees on green Lego grass.

The row of picture-perfect Georgian houses on Quality Row, Government House, the old penal colony administration buildings, and the ruins of the prisoners' compounds all look like props from a historical war-strategy simulation. Annie and Mitch half-expected to see actors in period costume storm out in mock battle.

Here, the primary colours competed for dramatic effect. The sky, always changing, but currently light blue. The sea, azure with deepening patches of navy. The island, every shade of green, from stark, dark pines to fluorescent lime grass. And the settlement buildings – all a proper colonial mellow yellow.

This area, Kingston, is the original settlement of Norfolk Island. But all Mitch and Annie see is a well-tended green lawn of a sharp-edged colonial civilisation, trying to stay calm amid the infinite forces of the wild and erotic, deep, blue nature.

They kept saying, "Oh wow" and "beautiful," while George watched them and remembered – like he did every time he brought a visitor to this spot – the awe of seeing it as a kid. Back when he first realised the incredible beauty of his home.

Even though as a child he'd never been anywhere else, George had known he was lucky. Norfolk was a kid's paradise to explore alone or by playing pirates with mates. He loved every blade of grass. Every ripple of wave. Every bird in every tree. They were all his. And he was theirs.

Now, he watched Mitch and Annie and saw it through their eyes. That infinite ocean. So blue. He stepped from the driver's door and moved closer to them.

They asked about the islands. George named them, slowly melting his frosty façade, and pointed out the buildings, the reef, and the pier.

"Most of the large freight comes ashore over there," he said, pointing to the pier, "but it has to be calm. Come on I'll show you," and led them back to the ute.

They drove down the rutted road with its immense Pacific view. There were cows grazing on the side of the road, or lounging on the grass, chewing cud, like old baseball coaches chewing tobacco. Or some were just standing still, admiring the scenery.

Around the next turn, a large brown cow sauntered across the road to chew the grass on the opposite verge. Its huge body blocked half the road causing George to a stop. They waited. Then, steering behind the animal, they drove slowly on.

"And *that* is how it's done," he said.

"Ow!" said Mitch wincing.

George smiled slightly and raised his eyebrows. Annie giggled awkwardly and shook her head.

At the next turn, the newlyweds were all eyes. The steep-roofed, slate-tiled houses looked like they'd been transplanted 20,000 kilometres from some quaint, British seaside towns to stand here, beneath a balmy Pacific sky. The Love Aliens stared in awe at straight-edged, angular buildings butting against the wild curves of nature; at reckless green hillsides lapped by the crystal reflections of ocean; and at this swirling blue world shrouded in the aura of a fine sea mist.

George showed them the pier and the humble manual crane that lifted every cube of cargo – including the ute they were sitting in – onto the island. But the water was so clear in the bay, and the reef so colourful with fish and coral, Mitch and Annie couldn't look at it long without wanting to take the plunge.

They drove to Emily Bay and parked above the curved beach and gazed over the calm water.

Annie asked, "Is it safe?"

George pointed to a large, yellow pontoon bobbing in the middle of the bay. They could see a person in green budgie-smugglers sunbathing on it.

"The local school has its swimming carnival here in Emily Bay," George said. "They start the swimming races on that pontoon. The kids dive off that and swim ashore."

That was enough for Mitch and Annie, who nodded and smiled to each other, then quickly went to the back of the ute. They each found a snorkel, mask and flippers, then stripped down to their togs.

That was enough for Blue, the dog, who asked politely to be released from his tether by panting loudly and pawing at Annie.

"Can I let Blue off the lead?"

"Yep," said George.

Annie unleashed Blue, who jumped down from the tray to regain his rightful seat in the cabin next to George.

Annie and Mitch fitted masks on their heads, with the snorkels dangling down their cheeks. Then they bent over and pulled flippers onto their feet. They stood, appraised each other, and laughed. Then Mitch pulled his mask down onto his face, plopped the snorkel into his mouth, snapped to attention and saluted.

Through his echoing snorkel, "Ready for action, Mrs Adams."

Annie pulled her mask down, inserted her snorkel, re-turned salute, and said through her snorkel, "Aye-aye, Captain Adams."

They turned to the water, locked arms, and – taking the goose-step back from the Nazis – walked down the sand, kicking their flippers up in front of them. After a few steps, Annie laughed aloud through her snorkel. Which did it for Mitch, too, who bent over and held his tummy. Their laughs funnelling from their snorkels sounded like the honking of ducks.

George smiled and shook his head, and said to Blue, "Dopey buggers. They should've waited until they were in the water to put their flippers on."

After a pause, he scratched Blue's ears, and said, "Yeah you're right, it wouldn't be as much fun that way."

Blue panted and they both looked at the duck people again.

George's friends, Muddy and Shaz, parked their car and walked to George's ute. The middle-aged couple in beach-wear made the Norfolk greeting, "Wataweih, George."

"Wataweih, Muddy," said George. "Wataweih, Shaz."

Muddy pointed to the couple still goose-stepping down to the water, and said, "Look at these dopey buggers."

"Should've waited 'til they were in the water to put their flippers on," said Shaz. "Everyone knows that."

George said, "Just said the same to Blue. But he reckons it looks like fun."

"You know 'em?" asked Muddy.

"Yeah—nah—," said George, "—sorta'."

Shaz said, "You showing 'em around?"

George said, "Yeah, Mum made me."

And they all shared a smile at the benevolence of the family matriarch.

Muddy asked, "Family friends?"

"Not really," said George, "they ran over Mildred."

Shaz said, "The cow?"

"She gonna be OK," asked Shaz.

"Dunno," said George, "She's with Candice now. Find out tomorrow."

"Bastards," said Muddy.

"Yeah—nah—," said George, "they're alright. Accident. Poor buggers really. Pair of touro lovebirds on their honeymoon."

"Too busy looking into each other's eyes, eh," said Shaz.

"Too busy feeling each other up," said Muddy.

Muddy and George giggled and Shaz slapped Muddy's shoulder.

CHAPTER ELEVEN

SUBMARINERS

In an act of heavenly compromise, God created coral reefs around Norfolk Island.

Sure, it stopped access for larger vessels, but it also provided one of the world's most perfect swimming bays. The coral reef protecting Emily Bay acts like a filter. It stops the big ocean waves and the sharks.

You can see the white line of foaming water where the reef protects the bay: wild Pacific Ocean on one side of the white line; and calm protected lagoon on the other.

At high tide, the ocean brims over the reef, but even during huge surf the bay is comparatively calm. Days like today, when the ocean's peaceful and the tide is low, the bay is tranquil as a pond.

Mitch and Annie waddled into the shallows, clutching their masks and snorkels, and sloshing awkwardly until they couldn't lift their flippers above the surface. They turned to walk backwards, and instead, promptly fell over.

The cool water clenched their pores. Bubbles obscured their underwater view. Spluttering, they raised their wet heads above the water, laughing at each other. Then they fixed their masks and snorkels and submerged. Immediately an alien underwater world opened up to them.

Like aquamarine glass, the water was clear and shallow with sunlight reflecting off the sandy bottom of the bay. It remained sandy for the first 50 metres or so, then the coral outcrops appeared.

The pair snorkelled deeper into the bay, threading through a channel between coral reefs where the water gradually intensified into a richer deep blue. The water was so clear, visibility seemed endless. The colours of the hard and soft corals – bright orange, yellow, pink, red, green, brown and purple – were vibrant to the limits of their vision.

Sunlight reflected off the channel's sandy floor, forming two strips of aquamarine, top and bottom, with a band of lapis lazuli across the middle. It looked like a flag for some underwater country.

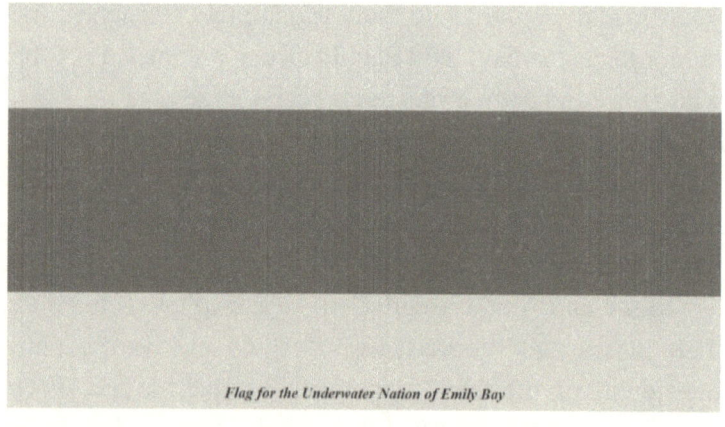

Flag for the Underwater Nation of Emily Bay

As they swam further, the coral outcrops grew in colour, complexity, and size. They found themselves in an exotic garden, sprouting flowers and plants from an alien world.

The birds and bees of this alien world floated between the coral "flowers": butterflyfish in gold and white stripes; wrasse with neon-blue lightning bolts; and dainty pouting damselfish flashing their orange and blue frills.

The towers of coral sprouted magnificent anemones on their surface; their internal subway system of intersecting tunnels made them more like an underwater city than a garden.

Each coral bommie was home to a territorial aatuti (damselfish) – scaly purple, orange and black – that chased off intruders from its area, like a guard dog protecting its home. Each block of reef was blessed with Norfolk cardinalfish, organised by a sergeant major, entertained by a blue drummer. Each complex had a surgeonfish operating, an eastern footballer playing, and a goatfish eating anything it could find.

Every suburb knew members of the notorious wrasse family: there was doubleheader wrasse and surge wrasse – the leaders; cigar wrasse, green moon wrasse, and knife wrasse – the gangsters; inscribed wrasse – the writers; luculent wrasse – the models; sixbar wrasse and threespot wrasse – the musicians; and skulking away in the shadows, weedy surge wrasse – the deviants.

In the basement of each coral development, a shy porcupinefish lived in its own secluded apartment, like a socially awkward, bumbling bachelor.

Lower still, the nocturnal morays and secretive snake eels were hiding away, deep within the dark alleys of the coral catacombs. Like underworld bosses ruling the night, they rarely left their subversive, submarine dens.

Flying majestically through the whole city were the green sea turtles. Calm and wise, they seemed like the true rulers of this alien world, overseeing it all from their shelled spaceships.

And right at the ceiling of this hydrosphere, swam Annie and Mitch, like alien satellites of love surveying from the sky. They snorkelled their own air from another world, and splashed their fake fish-fins, while staring down goggle-eyed at it all.

Sometimes, they'd dive straight down, to peer closely at the tame tropical fish. They pointed for each other to see the intricate weaves of red and yellow coral. When they found themselves unexpectedly surrounded by a school of garfish – the patterns of interleaved fish shapes swimming around them like an M.C. Escher zoetrope – they reached out to touch each other's white bodies on the arm or leg. Just to share the moment. Just to reassure themselves that this alien world was actually real.

The rest of the time, these two Love Aliens floated, watching the delicate, vibrant fish suspended in their swimming ether. And they felt safely held there, together in a fluid womb. Mr and Mrs Adams finally felt like they were at home, on their own Love Alien planet.

They swam down deep and felt the thermocline change at different depths. And their skin tingled in anticipation.

Then, swimming over the tops of shallow reefs, they sucked in their bellies and flippered gently, so they didn't knock the roofs of the coral skyscrapers. They followed a yellow butterflyfish in about 30 centimetres of water, where the sun's warmth reflected off the colourful coral. They felt the sunlight shining on their bare backs and reflecting up to their bellies. A sandwich of sun's warmth in the cool water.

As they followed the cheeky yellow fish into a clearing, they saw rainbow lines of refracted sunlight dancing across the sandy bottom.

The butterflyfish casually entered a hole in the coral, like it was entering a doorway of a building. Annie and Mitch rested their flippers on the sandy bottom and stood in shoulder-height water.

Their body heat transmitted across the touch of their skin. It came across from Annie's fingertip to Mitch's arm; from his hand to her waist; from chest to chest; from thigh to thigh; and from lips along necks, in the way of enthralled lovers. Before long, it buzzed between their lips and between their embracing bodies.

Their warm mouths, kissing in the cooler water was a sensation they relished. And their tongues twisted and twirled, around each other, like mating seahorses. Then they both rose and gasped for breath, and smiled and laughed together, breathless. Then locked again.

On the reef between Emily Bay and the Pacific Ocean, between civilisation and raw nature, between safety and danger, in the calm private world of Annie and Mitch – and a thousand tropical fish – they made like honeymooners and experimented.

It was more about the trying. About experiencing the undeniable drive, and the divine cosmic attraction that made them try.

Soon their masks were gone, their togs were down, or aside, and the only things keeping them afloat were their flippers, their stroking arms, and their lust for life.

At times, their passion was so strong and immediate, it seemed they'd die to complete the act. Then survival instinct kicked in and one would swim to the surface and gasp.

Then the other would pop up, but now with no laughter. Just wry smiles and iris eyes and quick fingers and gasping breath, as they went down, again.

They swirled together like a pair of sea nymphs with streaming hair in the diffused light from above. Their flippers flapping and legs wrapping and arms slapping.

The Love Aliens achieved the impossible for normal humans for a startling moment of pure ecstasy. A marital coupling that would've been the special moment they'd recall with a sparkle in their eyes for the rest of their lives. And admittedly, according to all the community of fish – who can judge a sensation by its vibrational waves – a moment that achieved the highest peak of human sensation on their fish Sense-O-Meter. But also a moment that may have been the instant of conception of their first child, were it not for two concurrent events:

1. The wedding ring slipped off Annie's finger.

2. The glass-bottom boat turned and puttered into Emily Bay.

Interestingly, the glass-bottom boat is pronounced *glaas botham boet* in the Norf'k language. And you'd think, with all those tourists staring through the viewing window at Annie and Mitch's writhing nakedness, that the glass-bottom boat (however you want to pronounce it) would've been the prick that deflated Annie and Mitch's ultimate ecstasy. But no, the glass-bottom boat was actually helpful. It was that gold wedding ring that came back to bite them.

Here's why.

The moment Annie's wedding ring was dislodged from her ring finger, sensory neurons on the surface of her skin alerted her somatosensory cortex. Something, somewhere deep in Annie's amygdala, registered the movement.

So strong was her connection to Mitch, so deep her commitment to their marriage, and so deep the symbolism of that connection, that the alarm rose through the orgy of instincts at play in that moment of highlight peak sensation.

Her motor cortex succeeded in sparking Annie's peripheral attention for a millisecond. But then the pleasant chorus of affective touch sensations drowned out the alarm about the ring in a clamour of sensual, submarine self-interest.

Then the ring came off, and the sensory neurons on the tip of Annie's finger projected the loss. The alarm resurfaced in Annie's motor cortex with such immediacy, she gasped mid-copulation and looked down to her ring, only to see it falling through the water.

By reflex, Annie swirled her hand to catch it. The current of movement slowed the ring's descent and also drew Mitch's attention. But the ring flipped and descended quickly – like a gold ring through water – past the layers of the coral complex and into a hole at the bottom of the reef.

The couple surfaced and gasped, and Annie spluttered, "My ring!"

Mitch gulped a breath and dived.

It was still only seconds after they'd been ecstatically interlocked, and the crucial appendage in Mitch's anatomy was still aptly activated. But nothing stops a Love Alien! So, with no mask, togs around his knees, and swelling with a stiff rudder, Mitch dived down, over a ledge of coral, to the sea floor. He swam around the Gaudian architecture for a moment, then thrust his hand into the hole where the ring had gone.

The cavern underneath this hole just happened to be the den of one of Emily Bay's most feared yet misunderstood nocturnal inhabitants, the banded or harlequin snake eel, Rocco. (Myrichthys colubrinus.)

Initially, Rocco had been amused by the golden ring falling into his den. He'd gone to inspect. But it was past his bedtime, and he'd been disinclined to investigate further.

He was retreating, back into the sandy bottom of his den to resume his sleep, when suddenly, he saw Mitch's hand poking into his hole.

Rocco the banded snake eel immediately turned to retreat through the rear passageway of his kingdom. But as he exited, he encountered another strange, one-eyed eel, coming hard at him.

Assuming it was an all-out attack by this strange, pink eel, Rocco defended his territory with the only weapon a banded snake eel has – the two rows of teeth that run along his jaws. Fortunately for Mitch, the banded snake eel's teeth aren't as sharp as a moray eel's. Unfortunately for Mitch, they're still teeth.

Also, unfortunately for Mitch, those teeth bit the head of his penis, which had – less than a minute earlier – registered a lifetime peak of ecstasy on the aquatic Sense-O-Meter.

Now, within that very same minute, Mitch was subjected to not just the greatest pain in his own lifetime, but the greatest pain in the cellular memory of his human DNA. (Including the 1724 torture of Mitch's great-great-great-great-grandfather by the Spanish Inquisition.)

So painful, it made the residual DNA of the intervening generations wince.

So painful, it made all the fish, all the living coral, and all four green sea turtles in Emily Bay, shudder from the sympathetic disharmony of the vibrational shockwaves.

So painful, it even shocked Rocco the banded snake eel into unlocking his jaws.

So painful, it made Mitch shriek an explosion of bloody bubbles.

Which made Annie scream and wave for help.

Which made the *glaas botham boet* speed towards her.

Which made Mr Rogers, holidaying from Bendigo, lose his wide-brimmed, imitation Australian Cricket Team hat over the side of the boat. But later that day, the hat floated into shore where it was found and photographed and posted onto social media by #DarrenTheBaron under the title: 'Hat found Emily Bay' #LotsaFlotsam. #Howzat #CricketHat-Caught. The post was seen by Mr Rogers's wife, Irene, who claimed the hat. So at least that part of the story ended well. The rest, though, was thoroughly horrific.

They hoisted screaming Mitch onto the *glaas botham boet* with all the tasteful delicacy of a B-grade horror movie set in a war zone. Near a nudist colony. With a slasher/flasher serial-killer surgeon operating in the field hospital. A clumsy surgeon. And it's filmed with hand-held shaky camera. With bad sound-effects but real blood.

Or even better, it's more like the director is actually a real-life serial killer. And it's a doco he's making with his brother, who's a real-life butcher. And also a serial killer. And somehow there's fish involved because there's a lot of footage shot from fishes' POV through the glass bottom of the boat.

OK. Come to think of it, you'd be hard up finding an equivalent sight as this one; with passengers screaming and falling over one another to help the naked snorkeller aboard, or else flipping overboard to get as far away from him as possible.

Fiasco is an understatement, but we'll spare you the gruesome details. Except to assure you that when they dragged that pale, screaming man into the *glaas botham boet* from the red water, his togs were caught around his flippers, and blood streamed from his groin. But fortunately, there was no banded snake eel still attached to his appendage.

Rocco had released his prey immediately after the attack. Whether it was through shock or not, you'd need to ask a marine-biology psychologist. Sadly, psychology is a vastly underfunded area of marine biology. Which is a tragedy in itself but probably not as immediate as the one speeding towards the perfect beach of Emily Bay in the *glaas botham boet*, with a screaming man surrounded by wide-eyed tourists who got more sightseeing than they'd paid for.

You'd know, if you're a marine biology psychologist, that before Rocco whizzed back into his den, he felt, possibly for the first time in banded snake eel history, a flash of guilt.

Meanwhile, the ambulance was at the shore when the *glaas botham boet* nosed up the beach with its new passengers. It's no coincidence that the two paramedics waiting on the beach were the same two who'd attended the cow crash 20 hours earlier, because there aren't many ambos on Norfolk Island.

Mitch was shrieking in agony, the boat was awash with blood, and Annie was pushing a towel against Mitch's groin. You've never seen passengers depart a boat so quickly.

They didn't even wait for the skipper to slide the gangplank ashore. They piled over the gunwales and splashed into the waist-deep water. Some were graceful but not many. Most slipped and splashed and bellyflopped into the water. But far from riotous, it was the quietest, most respectful mass exodus you've seen from a floating vessel in distress.

The ambos carried the empty stretcher down the beach, up the gangplank, across the bow, along the deck, and laid it next to the wailing man. But Mitch couldn't be rolled, so putting him in the stretcher wasn't an easy operation on the rocking boat. The ambos stood, swaying, while Annie swabbed and sobbed, and Mitch flat-out screamed.

The two paramedics, Greg and Steve, had been mates on Norfolk Island since birth. They'd gone to kindy together. And primary school. And high school. And cubs, scouts, footy, fishing, cricket, surfing, scuba diving, horse riding, and everything else kids do on Norfolk Island.

They'd been present at each other's every birthday, including Greg's ill-fated eighth birthday party where Steve kissed Greg's sister, Lorelei. The two boys had started fighting each other, but as soon as they'd punched each other once, they both cried – not because they were hurt but because they'd hurt their best mate. Then they'd hugged and sworn off girls. (Steve later married Lorelei.)

A year ago, they'd both completed their Diplomas of Paramedical Science and Emergency Health Care in Brisbane and returned to Norfolk Island.

Now they eyed each other along Mitch's shrieking, bloody form, and nodded.

They bent down together in perfect sync. Greg reached under Mitch's shoulders while Steve grabbed the screaming man's ankles. They looked up again, into the eyes of their lifelong friend at the other end of this atrocity, and nodded. Then gently lifted Mitch onto the stretcher.

They nodded to each other once more and lifted the stretcher, swaying together in time with the rocking boat.

Greg walked backwards along the deck carrying the stretcher handles, and Steve walked forwards carrying the other end. Both glanced down at the viewing window of the *glaas botham boet* and noticed the sloshing vomit splattered on the glass in front of some curious fish looking up at them. But they weren't distracted from their task as they edged further along the deck to the bow stairs. They went up the steps and across the bow, one shaky step at a time, then started along the gangplank.

It didn't have to move much. Not even a centimetre. But the shift was enough to jolt Greg's footsteps on the slippery gangplank and spill him and Steve, with Mitch still on the stretcher, sideways into the shallow water.

Annie's scream scared birds from their perches a kilometre away. In the national park, a rare green parrot flew from its hiding spot and gave Margaret King's Birdwatchers' Tour a photo frenzy. Out at Two Chimneys Reserve, white terns flew from the Norfolk pine forest like an explosion of sparks. And closer by, at Cemetery Bay, a great cormorant dropped its dinner back into the drink and didn't even try to retrieve it. He just flew.

Fortunately, Mitch fainted so his pain was nullified. But the poor ambos were splashing in bloody chaos, and the distressed tourists on the beach cried loudly and hugged each other. Annie of course, was frantic. Even so, she immediately jumped into the water to assist.

But it was Don, the boat driver, who was most affected. He hadn't seen so much blood and vomit since 1991, serving in Iraq with British forces. He was shocked back to that trauma now and stood with his left hand on the steering wheel of the *boet*, his mouth ajar and his right-hand twitching at his side.

Then a great cormorant flew overhead and broke Don from his trance. And just like that, he snapped into action and dived from his boat into the splashing melee of blood, ambos, Mitch, stretcher, and Annie.

Don rose from the shallows wearing Mitch on his back, like a backpack, and jogged like that up the beach to the ambulance.

Then it was everyone else's turn to stand still and stare with their mouths ajar. The only person to move was #DarrenTheBaron, who filmed the miraculous rescue on his phone. He posted it online with the tags: 'Spectacular Beach Rescue' #DarrenTheBaron #BeachRescue #NorfolkIsland #TourGuideHero #BloodyPenis.

In the shallows, Annie washed blood out of her hair then ran up the beach to George in his ute.

George had been dozing in the cabin until the arrival of the ambulance sounding its siren had woken him. Some instinct immediately told him that the emergency was related to the snorkelling honeymooners.

CHAPTER TWELVE
HOSPITAL

Norfolk Island Hospital was built by the New Zealand army during World War II, to recuperate Kiwi soldiers returning from conflict in the Coral Sea. The single-storey pine construction had originally housed two doctors' consulting rooms, a nurses' station, administration, and one small ward consisting of two beds.

In the intervening 80 years, it'd been extended with eight consulting rooms, a day surgery, an intensive care unit, pathology, radiology, and additional buildings for an ambulance station, dental clinic, psychologist's suite, physiotherapist's clinic, kitchen, maintenance sheds, and an aged-care facility – known as "Daa Randa" because it was originally an enclosed verandah and the name had stuck.

Now, the hospital compound covered two lush acres of low buildings connected by covered walkways. The place buzzed with twelve admin staff, ten nurses, ten maintenance crew, ten kitchen staff, five doctors, four paramedics, three gardeners, a dentist, a psychologist, an OT, and a physio.

And even though the drive from Emily Bay to the hospital in a speeding ambulance is less than five minutes, even before the ambo had arrived at the compound most of those 58 people knew all the details of Mitch's injury. Within an hour, their families knew, too. Here's how:

Greg, the ambo, had radioed ahead to the triage nurse. The triage nurse told the chief medical officer, who told the other doctors, who told the other nurses, who told the receptionists, who told all the people in the waiting room, who told their phones.

Most of the conversations went like this one, between Sarah the nurse and her uncle, Bunny Adams, the hospital's chief gardener:

Nurse Sarah has fair hair, fine skin and sentimental eyes. She wears a crisp white uniform as she walks across the manicured green lawn from the emergency entrance towards Bunny, who, as well as being the chief gardener for 30 years, also plays Captain Bligh in the weekly stage play *Mutiny* and was co-founding member of the a cappella group, Choral Reef.

Bunny is short and wiry, with a deeply tanned face and startling blue eyes. He's removed his wide-brimmed Norfolk-plait hat to admire the Pacific sky overhead. A smile twitches his lips because the bright clouds against the blue sky remind him of a Matisse collage.

Nurse Sarah approached him saying, "*Wataweih Unka.*" ("Hello, uncle.")

"*Ah, wataweih myse niece.*" ("Ah, hello my niece.")

"*Ess emergency, unka, bata clear dar driwe,*" said Sarah. ("It's an emergency, uncle, better clear the driveway.")

"Foot dar?" said Bunny. ("OK, why's that?")

"Sumthing se bite guy orna pulla," said Sarah. ("Something bit a guy on the knob.")

"Dar hawa hutt," ("That's gotta hurt,") said Bunny, wincing as he walked away to move his vehicle from the emergency driveway.

The impressive transfer rates of information that day wasn't just another example of Norfolk Island's famous *"dem tell'* ("they say") or small-town gossip. This one's a phenomenon known well to triage nurses everywhere.

The speed of a hummingbird's wings, the transfer of electrons, even the speed of light, all come in second place to the human impulse to share news about an injury to someone else's genitalia. (Conversely, the slowest transfer rate is news about injury to one's own genitalia.)

Fortunately for Mitch, the morphine administered by the ambos had taken effect and he was unaware of his celebrity status. He wasn't even aware he was being pushed on a gurney from the ambulance into the hospital.

Mitch was slightly aware of gooiness in his mid-section and warmth at his temples, but he attributed that to the thrill of zooming with Annie through the golden wedding rings of Saturn on a rollercoaster eel.

Annie on the other hand, running behind the gurney towards the hospital entrance, noticed everything.

The gurney's rubber tyres crunching gravel on the driveway.

The awkward fluttering of a palm frond in the soft breeze to her left.

The surprisingly high number of staff present to facilitate their entry to the building.

A data sample of the staff's facial expressions by percentage:

- 42% concerned;
- 26% sad;
- 18% horrified;
- 10% fascinated;
- 4% other.

The perfect circle of a dandelion poking up from the lawn.

The height of the lip of the ramp compared to the radius of the trolley wheels.

The width of the gurney compared to the emergency entrance doorway.

The swoosh of air as they ran through the doors.

The corridor lined by staff.

The different uniforms of the numerous staff.

The smooth sound of rubber wheels rolling over linoleum flooring.

The khaki colour of the corridor walls behind the numerous staff.

The generous width of the timber boards in the 1942 construction.

The emptiness of the waiting room.

The synchronised footsteps of the paramedics pushing the gurney between the walls of staff.

But none of these details even dented Annie's hyper-vigilant focus in its peak crisis mode. Until she noticed one woman's face, among the tunnel of staff lining their path to emergency.

It was the incongruity that made Annie glance twice at her.

For a start, the woman was dressed like a receptionist, in a lavender twinset with a black business skirt, spectacles, and a telephone headset straddled over her neat bun.

Which all seemed out of place in an emergency. But it was the way the woman was chewing gum while pointing her phone to film Mitch on a gurney, that shattered Annie's concentration.

And for the first time since the accident, Annie registered the specific physical location of her new husband's injury. The effect was "spectacular" (according to #DarrenThe Baron who was capitalising on his new fame as a social-media journalist and filming the procession).

In #DarrenTheBaron's now-famous footage, we see an ambulance gurney pushed by two paramedics along a khaki-coloured corridor lined with bystanders. A fit young woman with wet blonde hair and wearing a yellow bikini is running behind the gurney.

Suddenly, the woman in yellow bikini changes direction, like a shark, swerving away from the gurney to attack a woman in a lavender twinset and black office skirt.

Before anyone notices, the bikinied woman is behind the innocent bystander, and pushing her forwards by the neck, shouting, "Get a good eyeful? Pervert!"

Then the yellow bikini woman is rag-dolling her cardiganed puppet along the corridor, trailing the gurney, yelling, "Wanna closer look, pervert? Do ya?! Do ya?!"

The unfortunate victim's conservative office composure is demolished immediately. Her arms and legs are flailing, headset and spectacles are flying, hair-bun is sprung loose, and her left high-heel shoe is spinning through the air.

The other staff are seen moving quickly to arrest the attack, including the paramedic who's pushing the gurney from the rear. He swings his head to the disturbance on his left, and when he sees the two women careering towards him, he skips forwards and ankle-taps the rear-wheel of the speeding trolley.

In one quick movement, the gurney twists sharply, wobbles erratically, and flips the patient in a short arc onto the polished lino floor.

The slow-motion footage of Mitch flying off the gurney and slamming onto the linoleum, became the most popular meme across all social media apps, with the subtitle, "So you think you're having a bad day".

The footage of Annie shaking the innocent bystander, and shouting, "Take a closer look, pervert" became the most posted clip in the world for two months. Then it made a resurgence for another month, when it was sub-titled, "Me before my coffee".

The footage was played across the entire alphabet of TV news stations – from ABC, BBC, and CNN, all the way to XXP, YLE, and ZTV.

The hospital near Kingston, Norfolk Island, was discussed on daytime talk shows from Kingston, Jamaica, to Kingston, Ontario.

It was analysed on night-time panel shows in Kingston, New York, Missouri, Oklahoma, Rhode Island, Pennsylvania, Texas, Oregon, New Mexico, Kentucky, Alabama, Ohio, and Washington.

Social-commentary TV shows cited Annie's behaviour as an example of "the insanity of modern life" by experts on everything from low-fat diets and high anxiety to gender bias and swimsuits.

Stand-up comedians, and comedy shows like *The Late Show* and *Saturday Night Live*, parodied the footage for so long that "Yellow Bikini woman" became cultural shorthand for "sexy but crazy".

In music, #DarrenTheBaron's phone footage was edited into a film clip for three top-selling songs. Firstly, by Sia and Harry Styles for their collab hit, "Crazy 4 U". Then, by jazz-metal outfit, DeMentor for their indie ballad, "Bad Bad Bad Day". And finally, and most irritatingly, by teen Swiss one-hit-wonder Young Maestro for his novelty hit "Yellow-Bikini Bat-shit Babe".

But all that was yet to come, in the hours, days and months after the actual event took place in Norfolk Island's hospital.

Back then, in that khaki-coloured corridor, in that screaming moment of wheeling hysteria, when Annie was holding a stranger in a headlock. And her husband of 48 hours was flying through the air. And everyone else's face was wrenched in shock because their sympathetic nervous system was ejaculating adrenaline into their bloodstream. Back then, when chaos was peaking, it was the quiet way Mitch groaned after landing, that snapped Annie out of her madness.

"Ooof," said Mitch.

Annie suddenly released the receptionist and skidded along the floor to Mitch, and said, "Darling, darling, I'm so sorry."

The paramedics urged her aside and lifted Mitch back on the gurney. Then nodded to each other and continued towards emergency at pace.

Annie watched them from the floor, while behind her the other staff recomposed their fallen colleague. When the gurney finally passed through the flapping door of emergency, Annie turned and started to make an apology to the defiled bystander.

Her words turned into uncontrollable sobbing so violent that the staff left their colleague to attend to the new "code yellow" medical condition of Annie's hyperventilation. And the wretched receptionist was left to wilt softly into the nearest chair.

CHAPTER THIRTEEN
WAITING ROOM

George had missed the action. He was still in the hospital car park sitting in the cabin of his ute scratching Bluey between the eyebrows.

"Well, we dropped her off," said George to the dog. "We can go home now, right mate? Job done, yeah?"

Bluey tilted his head at George, then looked over to the hospital entrance.

George followed the dog's gaze, then shook his head and crossed his arms and looked out his window, 'Why should I go in?' he said. "I don't even know 'em!"

Then looking back at Blue, George said, "They ran over Mildred. You know that? Right?"

Blue's eyebrows dented, then he smiled and panted.

"Oh, shut up," said George, and ruffled the dog's brow and they smiled at each other.

Mary had entrusted George with a duty to take the newlyweds swimming. His mother would expect him to follow through no matter where it led. It was Bluey's smile that'd reminded him of this hapless duty.

George stepped out of the cabin and walked towards the hospital entrance. Bluey jumped out the passenger window and trotted in the opposite direction to a grove of shady trees at the far end of the car park.

George entered the khaki-coloured corridor and said hello to the ladies in admin. He'd known most of them his whole life so was a bit surprised that they were all too engrossed in their busy chatter to respond to him.

He kept walking along the lino tiles to the waiting room and reception counter. Most of the staff were there, buzzing around Annie like bees around a hive. Some were patting her, some were talking gently, one was taking her pulse, one was pumping a blood-pressure bandage, another was holding her teacup, another was offering her a biscuit.

George laughed, and they all swung around at him with such stinging looks that he immediately apologised.

Then, quietly from the heart of the hive, Annie asked, "George?"

The nurses, who'd all known George for decades, swung their heads from George back to Annie, then back to George to hear his answer.

"Yes, it's me," he said to the queen, back there somewhere in the hive. Then to the worker bees around her, George said, "She's Mum's friend."

"Oh," they said as one, then eagerly handed over their tools of caring.

George was suddenly laden with a cup of tea and a plate of biscuits, then ushered to the seat next to Annie. A clipboard of paper forms was laid on his lap and a pen was inserted behind his ear. Then, the staff were gone in a hushed shuffle of wafer-soled loafers on linoleum tiles.

Sitting there, in the khaki waiting room, George found himself in a unique position. Not only was his arm around a stranger's sobbing shoulders. But it was a stranger he'd detested only a few hours earlier.

The irony wasn't lost on George, and initially he couldn't breathe properly. Then he looked down at Annie, and his dark eyes warmed, and the famous Norfolk Island kindness was restored. He sighed a deep breath and relaxed his arm around her shoulders, while Annie's head nuzzled into George's chest.

Annie had stopped sobbing now, and just seemed exhausted from the exertion of panic and violence. With her eyes closed, she was curled up into the crook of George's arm, her hands clasped together in a pillow, or a prayer.

George was newly uncomfortable. Not just because he was balancing a plate of biscuits in his hand and a cup of tea in the other.

Like many Norfolk Island men, his tough, bronzed exterior was wrapped around the most beautifully soft, warm, generous heart. A caring man, he'd spent more than his fair share of nights comforting his kids, or calming his wife, or consoling his mates. But never with a body so foreign.

The difference between holding a loved one and holding a stranger is the warmth. You connect with the warmth of a loved one, fired in the kiln of a million instances. Of laughs, tears, grazes and apologies, and of years and years of ups and downs.

With a stranger, it can feel like you're holding a statue.

But over time, and tears, and Annie's enormous need, her body had grown warm by his side. And George began to take a paternal care for the young lady.

He felt her breathing moving against him, and became aware of his own chest, expanding and deflating against her cheek.

He looked down at her soft face, resting against his chest, and a smile twitched his cheeks. He was genuinely happy that she was finally calm.

Then his eyes flicked around the waiting room and over the reception counter, but no one was around.

George was born in this tiny island town so had learnt early to be careful of people getting the wrong idea. Gossip here, in this little floating community, was especially virulent.

George needn't have worried.

By now, an hour after the accident, everyone in the first ring of the island's social circle – about 300 out of the 2,000 inhabitants – already knew of Annie and her honeymooning husband. Within another hour, the second ring of 600 people would know. And by the next day, the third ring would know the story. (The fourth ring of social outcasts never knew anything anyway because they were uncontactable, or worse, didn't listen to gossip.)

The story of a man being bitten on the penis by a banded snake eel was being savagely distorted in the retelling. But the closest-to-truth gossip that was currently contaminating the island was that Mitch's entire appendage had been amputated by the chomping bite of a:

- sea snake

- moray eel

- rock cod.

Never mind that the banded snake eel is neither sea snake nor moray eel. (And not even in the same genus as a rock cod.) Never mind that the open mouth of the banded snake eel is about 18 millimetres in diameter. Never mind that its bite has a maximum of four teeth punctures. Never mind the facts – the first victim in gossip is the truth.

There were at least two more fantastic and more salacious variants of the story spreading around the cafés and kitchen of the island.

In one, it was Annie (not a sea snake, moray eel, or rock cod) who had bitten off Mitch's most private appendage in a fit of passion.

But the story gathering the most airplay was the most predictable, and the most sordid extension of the truth. In this gossip, the morning's two incidents had become entwined and Roz, the ill-fated receptionist, was not such an innocent bystander.

In this version:

- Roz the receptionist had an affair with Mitch. ("On the first night of his honeymoon!")

- Annie discovered the infidelity and bit Mitch's knob completely off. ("Understandably.")

- Then Annie had attacked Roz at the hospital. ("Also understandably.")

Perfect.

Picture a map of the small heart-shaped island. It's eight-kilometres at its longest point and five-kilometres wide.

A TV graphic would use three different coloured lines to show the dissemination of these three stories around the island.

The truest story is a blue line, the first variant is green, and the perfectly sordid fiction is red.

You'd see the blue lines starting quickly and pulsing along the main veins of the heart-shaped map. Then the green lines would take over and flow more quickly from there, filling up the arteries. Then the red lines of adultery and revenge would flood the rest of the map in a surge of speeding lines.

So, sitting in the waiting room, George needn't have worried about people getting the wrong idea. They already had the wrong idea. A variety of them. But none were the wrong idea he was afraid they'd get.

The prevailing wrong idea about George is:

- He's Annie's second cousin;

- Annie is the jilted newlywed who won't be jilted again;

- Mitch is the promiscuous newlywed whose jilting days are over;

- Roz, the receptionist, is the adulteress who took the wrong honeymooner to bed.

George and Annie, the unlikely couple who'd been through so much together, sat silently in the khaki-coloured waiting room. They were in the eye of a cyclone, completely unaware of the whirlwind of words spinning around them.

CHAPTER FOURTEEN
WEATHER

On the radio, the weatherman Henry "Vane" Thompson was waxing lyrical, "The unique weather patterns on Norfolk Island mean that it's sunny one minute, stormy the next. As moody as a toddler. And you never know which way it's going to go. Hysterical tantrums one minute; purest delight the next. But when it's smiling," he said, "it's like a revelation. When the sun is shining and the sky is blue on Norfolk Island, it'll make you want to take up painting."

CHAPTER FIFTEEN

LIFE AQUATIC

The only one unaffected by the incident in the bay, and the ensuing whirlwind of words, was the banded snake eel, Rocco.

He recovered quickly from the shock of the attack and was back in his den lying under a thin blanket of white sand, contemplating the gold wedding ring glistening before his eyes.

Rays of sunlight shone through the surface ripples of the bay, down through the holes in the coral, down into Rocco's den. Where they sparkled on that gold ring in the sand. It reflected around his den like a golden disco ball.

Far from delighted by the light show, the ring was messing with Rocco's head. But as any good marine biology psychologist would tell you – if there were any – it doesn't take much to mess with a banded snake eel's head. Their brain is the size of a ball-bearing. (And not a very bright one.)

The ring glowed gold and seemed to move with the refracted glints of sunlight. So, Rocco might've assumed it was a living organism.

The ring's arrival had woken Rocco from his daily nap. So maybe he was resentful of it.

The ring was also linked to his earlier home invasion, where Rocco had been attacked by the fleshy one-eyed intruder. Seeing it again may have re-traumatised the poor banded snake eel. (Who really knows about snake eel psychology?)

Whatever the reason, Rocco edged closer to the ring. He circled it twice, where it lay in the centre of his disco-lit coral den. Then Rocco opened his mouth as wide as possible (a diameter of 18 millimetres) and bit the 16-millimetre ring. Whole.

Any psychological trauma the ring might've previously caused Rocco was nothing compared to the digestive trauma it now inflicted upon the poor banded snake eel.

Open your mouth, now, as wide as possible. Wide. Then stretch it open a bit more, and keep it like that, even for a short time, and you'll understand Rocco's predicament.

Rocco's mouth was forced wide open around the ring. He certainly wasn't going back to sleep any time soon. This was a dangerous obstruction which forced Rocco to leave his den to physically work out the problem.

Rocco, the wide-mouthed banded snake eel, with the ring of gold teeth, dashed from his cave and weaved through the alleyways of his coral complex, then splashed out into the bright open spaces of Emily Bay.

He raced and twisted. He swam as fast as he could, then stopped abruptly, then swam forwards again. He swam furiously, with no care for destination, but solely concerned with dislodging the golden obstruction from his gaping mouth.

Rocco zoomed around the bay. He zipped through reefs, bumped off soft coral, and at one point even curled himself into a wheel and rolled along the sandy sea floor. This drew some attention from the other fish who'd never seen that manoeuvre before.

But it didn't work for the small snake eel, who – all things considered – had had one hell of a strange day. And it wasn't over yet. He still had a wedding ring to release from his jaws.

So he swam faster than he'd ever swum in his strange short life. Rocco felt a moment of elation at the speed he reached, just before he entered Wally, the kingfish's mouth.

The next thing Rocco felt was thumping into the insides of the kingfish's oesophagus. Which was a perfectly bizarre ending to a perfectly bizarre day.

And life.

CHAPTER SIXTEEN

WALLY

Wally the kingfish experienced a new sensation, too. Never had he swallowed anything so quickly. Or so completely.

It caused some digestive issues for this bigger fish. Which may have been some small consolation for Rocco the banded snake eel, were he not already dead.

If we could decipher a kingfish's facial gestures, we might've noticed the sneering grimace one exhibits at the onset of indigestion. But "kingfish facial study" is another under-researched area that'd benefit from marine biology psychology.

A professor of marine biology psychology could've glanced at Wally and told us that the kingfish was suffering massive ingestion stress. And while the kingfish brain is bigger than a banded snake eel's, he's certainly no Einstein.

Fish brain-size is about one-tenth the size of a bird or mammal of similar dimensions. So it doesn't take much to confuse a fish.

"Massive ingestion stress" is enough to disrupt the basic brain function that a kingfish requires for swimming, eating, defecating, reproducing, and avoiding danger.

Luckily for Brian, the 69-year-old retiree paddling his kayak just outside the reef of Emily Bay, it was this last aspect of Wally's diminished capacity that worked in his favour.

CHAPTER SEVENTEEN

BRIAN

Brian's a friendly, retired fitter and turner who'd moved to Norfolk Island with his wife, Susan, one year ago. His bright orange kayak was a retirement present from Susan and one he enjoyed paddling around the lagoon most days. Occasionally he'd even take it outside the reef. Trawling a fishing line behind the kayak was also one of Susan's ideas.

"You may as well tow a line while you're out there," she'd suggested. "Maybe you'll catch us a fish for dinner."

But Brian was no fisherman – as his year of fishless fishing could attest. He didn't know fish, or the things that attracted them to a hook. Even though his hand-made lure was a thing of beauty.

Brian's hand-made, shallow lure danced through the water behind his kayak with such gracious intent that it actually scared fish. (Ask a marine biology psychologist why. If you can find one.)

Brian had fashioned the fanciful critter out of steel and pine. He'd painted the small wooden eyes with swirls of blue, like the Buddha eyes of a Nepalese thangka. He'd constructed fins of aluminium gauze for hydro-dynamicity.

He'd used the metal lathe in the Norfolk Island Men's Shed to shape its sleek stainless-steel body. Then the whole beast had been welded together by a master of twisted metal with too much time on his hands.

More a submersible art-piece than a fish-catching device, this magnificent lure had failed to lure any fish before, and Brian wasn't expecting any to be stupid enough to fall for it today.

He was out there, beyond the reef, for the exercise of paddling. He was there for the exhilaration of feeling the enormous Pacific Ocean just millimetres beneath his tiny vessel. He was there for the sight of windward seabirds wobbling overhead. For the contrast of royal blue sea against dramatic red cliffs. And Brian was there for singing his favourite song, "My Island Home," by the Warumpi Band and Christine Anu, as loudly as possible.

So Brian was as surprised as anyone – well not Mitch or Annie, or Rocco the banded snake eel, or even the wrongly-accused receptionist, Roz. OK, Brian was far down the chain of surprise by this day's account, but still surprised – when his line tugged, and his kayak slowed, and he was wrought from his song by the realisation that he'd caught a fish.

And what a beauty! Admittedly a lucky catch – through the tail – but a catch all the same.

Having never caught a fish before, it took Brian five minutes to reel it in. Then another five to disentangle himself from the line. But only a few seconds to capsize his kayak.

It took Brian another few minutes to right his vessel, but then he got tied up in the fishing line again because the hooked fish started swimming around him.

Brian was lucky to survive. But 18 minutes, one capsized kayak, one near-drowning, and one short swim to the reef towing the oar, the kayak, and the tangled fishing line, was a small price to pay for the quarry – a 12-kilogram kingfish.

CHAPTER EIGHTEEN

NEVILLE

First, it was the blood. Then the slow clumsy reel-in of the wildly writhing kingfish that drew Neville's attention.

But Neville, the bronze whaler shark, had eaten a good breakfast of baitfish out by South-West Rock. He wasn't too fussed when a potential kingfish lunch was pulled off the menu by a fishing line from that irritating orange kayak that paddled along the reef most days.

But it was the second opportunity, when the kayak over-turned and the human was flailing around and entangling itself in the writhing kingfish, that was too good to miss.

Brian would later tell Susan he'd never been so afraid in his life. He thought the shark was coming for him. But any good marine dietitian will tell you, Brian was too big and too dangerous for a small shark's meal. As it was, the bronze whaler could only get his teeth around the head of the kingfish.

Brian's home-made lure stayed true. He'd swum to the reef, scarpered up onto it, pulled in his oar and the kayak, then reeled in the line. And there was his magnificent lure, hooked in the blood and guts at the rear section of the king-fish.

Brian pulled the flesh from the aerodynamic foil and found its hook running through a small jawbone of tiny teeth shaped into an "O" around a gold wedding ring.

Brian must've looked at that glinting gold circle of teeth for a full minute trying to understand it.

Then he looked out to sea, in the direction of the long-gone bronzer. Then back at the ring. Then towards Emily Bay, inside the reef, where some kids were swimming.

He considered calling the kids over to ask them to un-ravel the puzzle. Then Brian looked back down at the gold ring encircled by small teeth. He carefully unlooped the ring of teeth from the sharp hook of his home-made lure.

The gold ring with teeth clamped around it, slipped over the tip of his forefinger. Brian blew out his cheeks, shook his head, and whispered, "Well, fuck me."

CHAPTER NINETEEN

WAITING

Annie and George were doing what you do in a waiting room, when Dr Pete came out and told them Mitch was safe.

Dr Pete was a tall, thin, dour man with buzz-cut grey hair and brilliant green eyes. His voice was so low, it was as if he'd mined it in his feet, and it'd echoed all the way up his 6 4 body. The effort to pipe it all that way meant he had no energy left to vary the tone. His words floated on the bottom "D" note of a tenor saxophone, whether he was talking about love, grief, surgery, joy, palliative care, the snorkelling in Vanuatu, his wife, Lana, or the weather in Norway.

Dr Pete said, "Mrs—?"

Annie looked around the waiting room, remembered her new surname, then swung up to Dr Pete, and said, "Adams."

"Yes," said Dr Pete. "Your husband is safe."

Annie's full range of emotions had a millisecond's Mexican fiesta through her body. Her facial gestures performed a short but dramatic one-woman play.

Dr Pete said, "He's asleep but you can see him if you like."

Annie nodded and followed the long man but looked back at George, who smiled and pointed to himself and to his chair, to indicate that he'd wait. Annie smiled, turned, and hardened her features for the upcoming shock.

There was nothing to fear. In the ward, there was her handsome husband's sweet face. Eyes closed, tilted to the side, he was gently snoring and dribbling a bit.

Annie smiled sadly as she watched him and felt a pang of guilt as she remembered rousing him from a similar slumber the previous night.

God, was that only the night before?

Then her eyes drifted down his body to the arch of blankets covering a frame at Mitch's mid-section.

Dr Pete saw her looking, "That's so the blankets don't put pressure on the wound."

Annie nodded but winced at the word "wound".

Annie said, "Can I see?"

"There's nothing *to* see."

"What do you mean, 'nothing'?"

"Bandaged."

"But he's—?" Annie didn't know the word.

"He's intact?" said Dr Pete.

"Yes."

"Yes, he'll be fine," said Dr Pete. "Just some micro stitching. Very minor abrasion. He'll be fine."

"We're on our honeymoon."

"Yes, I was told. He'll be fine. The major concern is infection."

"Oh?"

"We'll have to keep him under observation for a day or two," said Dr Pete. "On a drip. Strong antibiotics."

"Oh yes, OK. So, he'll—?"

Dr Pete asked, "He'll—?"

Annie continued, "—be—?"

Dr Pete asked, "Be?" The doctor's mind ran through a triage of emergencies the young woman might be trying to ask: "Able to walk?"

Annie said, "Umh—"

Dr Pete asked, "Fever?"

"Umh—I mean yes, good. Phew! Right? But umh— I meant—Sorry it really doesn't matter," she said turning away.

Then it hit Dr Pete, "Oh, you mean sexually?"

"Oh?" said Annie, now embarrassed.

"Yes, he'll be fine."

"Active?" said Annie.

"Functional."

"Able to feel?" she asked.

Dr Pete wondered if the young woman was asking if the patient could have sex immediately on waking. He recalled his own honeymoon and considered that maybe she was.

"Not immediately on waking," said Dr Pete. "There'll be healing and, like I said, the risk of infection. But it's just a small graze. Very lucky really. Could've been much worse considering the location and the proximity to the arteries. Very lucky."

"Oh good," said Annie, suddenly realising the doctor thought she was considering jumping Mitch's bones right now. She wished she could slip behind the plastic curtain and disappear, like magic, and never talk about her husband's penis again. Ever.

But Dr Pete continued, "As it was, it wasn't much worse than a zipper entrapment."

"Oh good," said Annie, but her brow furrowed to shield her mind from imagining what that was.

"But, as I say," said Dr Pete, "an infection is really all we have to be careful about."

Annie suddenly dropped her head and wept. She went to her husband and hugged him and pushed her teary cheek to his dry, sleeping face.

"You might want to let him sleep," said Dr Pete.

"Yes," said Annie. But she was privately disappointed Mitch hadn't woken and shone his beautiful angel eyes and smiled his sleepy dopey smile at her. She kept it to herself and squeezed Mitch's soft hand and walked out of the ward with a happy heart and a slight skip in her step.

Her smile transferred instantly to George's face. And she said, "He's going to be OK. In here a day or two—under observation."

Then she clenched George's arm in hers and they walked to the exit together.

Bluey, sitting under the shady trees, saw the hospital doors open slightly and noticed his owner's arm was pushing the door. The dog bounded across the car park and was in the back of the ute before the hospital door had fully opened.

Then Bluey noticed George stop at the open door and turn back inside. Bluey's speckled grey-and-black head tilted to the right. Then he saw George emerge from the doors; Bluey's tail drummed on the aluminium tray of the ute.

George looked across at Bluey and waved his hand down. Bluey's tail stopped wagging, his shoulders drooped, and his rump slumped down on the ute tray.

Over there, at the door of the hospital, George leaned against the wall of the balcony, waiting.

Inside, Annie was talking to Dr Pete, who'd called after her as she and George were leaving. Dr Pete was looking down at her, saying, "I believe you were in an accident."

"A few scratches, that's all," said Annie.

"Still quite traumatic," said Dr Pete.

"Yes," said Annie. "It's been a heavy week—well, day and a half."

"And I believe you attacked one of my administrative staff," said Dr Pete.

"Oh, yes," said Annie, "I'm very sorry about that."

Dr Pete said, "If you need to talk to somebody, you can see the psychiatrist here at the hospital."

"Oh, right," said Annie. "No, umh, thanks. I'm fine"

Dr Pete pointed to another building, "She's just in that building. You go and make appointment there."

"OK," said Annie.

"OK," said Dr Pete, "Another thing, there'll be some costs."

"Oh?" said Annie.

"The emergency operation is covered by Medicare," said Dr Pete, "but there might be costs for on-going medication."

"Oh," said Annie.

"You can fix that up in admin," he pointed, "where Roz works. So that might be a good time to tell her you're sorry."

CHAPTER TWENTY
ROUNDS

Father Pat, part-time rent-a-car guy/part-time radio announcer/full-time priest, arrived for his weekly rounds of Norfolk Island Hospital and parked next to George's ute. He patted Bluey sitting on the tray back, then followed the dog's eyes to George standing on the balcony, leaning against the wall.

Pat and George are related in the usual Norfolk Island way. Third cousins by birth, brothers-in-law by marriage, tennis partners on Thursday night, bowls opponents Wednesday afternoons, and barbeque buddies most Sundays. A simple wave between them can relay a conversation of information.

Father Pat understood from the wave that George was waiting for someone, but it wasn't family, and it wasn't serious, but it was a minor inconvenience and he'd rather be fishing.

George didn't need the wave to know Father Pat would be doing his hospital rounds. It was 4 pm Wednesday. What else would he be doing?

Father Pat walked past the hospital entry to the covered walkway that led along the network of interconnected buildings to the last and most modern building in the compound, "Daa Randa."

Norfolk Island's aged-care facility is only ten years old, and the only hospital building made of concrete blocks. It rests at the back of the compound overlooking the rainforest valley.

Pat's weekly rounds were mainly visiting the eight elderly folk who lived in Daa Randa. There are rarely any patients staying in the main hospital, but today Pat also wanted to visit the honeymooner who'd been doing it tough. He'd be in Ward One. No one knew why it was called Ward One – there's only one ward. So it's a sure bet he'd be there.

The priest walked into Daa Randa and smiled at the nurses, then visited Maisie Buffett who'd known Pat since he was born. She used to babysit Pat when he was a kid. Now he loved doing the same for her, every week, even if it was just for 15 minutes.

They sat on the balcony together and held hands. Maisie had been a nurse towards the end of the war. Fell in love with a war-torn American. They'd had six kids, who gave Maisie twelve grandkids, who were all scattered to the four winds, far away from Norfolk Island.

At almost 100 years old, Maisie's perseverance was now her greatest burden. She'd long lost the power of speech, so she and Pat sat in silence, and looked out at the green forest undergrowth behind the building.

After a few minutes, Maisie giggled for no reason. A few minutes later, she started to cry. Father Pat stroked her hand gently, and Maisie slowed her sobs. Her lovely pale blue eyes glistened as she looked back up at Pat, and she smiled with such beauty that it threatened to break the old priest.

Instead, he squeezed Maisie's hand softly and smiled back at her with all his love. Pat nodded knowingly; not actually knowing what he was supposedly knowing. Then they looked back out at the small ferns and green leaves and the rich brown soil.

The wind blew the leaves of an ancient white oak. The branches swayed like they were waving goodbye, but the thick old trunk stayed solid as rock.

"Big winds coming, eh?" said Pat.

Maisie nodded.

Pat soon stood and kissed Maisie's paper-thin cheek. He felt the pressure of tears behind his eyes but breathed deeply and thought about God's eternal love. Then he turned and left the room.

Next, Father Pat dropped a box of Ferrero Rocher chocolates off to Alice Young, whom he'd also known forever. Alice used to be the Norfolk Island butcher and had been a tearaway in her day. Pat's mum had always been wary of Alice, saying the lady butcher knew a good rump when she saw one, and often had an eye on Pat's father's.

Now, Alice was 92 years old, but still as naughty as her health and the nurses would allow. As usual, she told Pat how handsome his father had been back in the day.

"Yes, Alice," said Pat, "and weren't you were a looker, too?"

"You bet I was," said Alice.

"Lucky my mum kept him locked away from you," said Father Pat.

"Lucky for who?" asked Alice and cackled a laugh that turned into a cough that racked her slight frame. Pat rested his hand on her shoulder.

"It's OK, auntie. You just relax your wild heart now," said Father Pat. "Let's have a little prayer together, eh. Would you like that, my love?"

Alice nodded. They bowed their heads; Alice was snoring before they got to "Amen".

Pat chatted with the nurses on his way out. They gave him grubby details about the honeymooner's injury, and the ruckus between Annie and Roz in the main building earlier. Father Pat listened enthusiastically and laughed with the nurses at the reckless humanity.

Father Pat said, "I'd better go visit the poor fella," and he bid farewell to the nurses then walked along the covered walkway to the main entrance of the hospital.

He stopped with George who summarised the series of events since Father Pat had dropped the honeymooners at the double-booked Airbnb.

At first, Father Pat chuckled and shook his head, but by the end of the story he was dumbfounded. He just stared, wide-eyed, at George, while pondering God's part in this human farce.

"A cyclone those two," said Pat. "I don't know whether to laugh or cry." Then he looked up and shook his head at the Matisse clouds puttering across the blue sky, and said, "Just pray I guess."

George said, "That's about all you can do, I reckon, Pat."

They entered the hospital together. Father Pat to see Mitch, and George to see Annie, who was standing at the reception desk across from Roz.

Annie's shoulders were slumped, as Roz loudly enumerated the cost of the various items on the invoice.

"And this is for medication not covered by Medicare," said Roz.

George glanced at Father Pat and shook his head, then moved to stand beside Annie.

Roz looked up and smiled at George, "Hi George," then she rolled her eyes towards Annie and returned to loudly narrating the hospital bill, "Now where was I?—Bandages, three rolls—"

"Hi Roz," said George. "Hi Annie, everything alright?"

Roz, the receptionist, went suddenly quiet. She looked up at the two, assessing the social dynamics. She smiled at George but the smile faltered when she realised there was connection between George and Annie. It meant there was connection between Annie and the island. It meant Roz's social superiority had just slipped a notch or two.

Roz started talking again but stuttered. Her status was slipping further and she adjusted her delivery from bullying to sycophantic, saying, almost sweetly, "bandages—the little ones—three rolls—...".

She was serving a shit-cake with polite icing. She'd passed straight over professional and landed on soft and sympathetic... and fake as a palm-reader's con.

Father Pat smirked in the background before walking down to Ward One. Mitch was still in Bed Two, and still unconscious.

Pat asked Nurse Sarah about the honeymooner's welfare. She told him the same story he'd heard twice in ten minutes. But this time it consisted of facts. Strangely, this version was even more incredible.

Father Pat shook his head at the wonder of it all. Marvelled at the complexity of this game of chance. Thought for a second that Mother Mary Christian-Bailey might be Lady Luck. Smiled to himself.

The heart of Father Pat's faith wasn't about how a loving God could let bad things happen to ones we love. No, with all the moving parts in an infinite universe, Father Pat wondered how any of us made it this far.

He walked back through the reception, smiling at Roz, George and Annie.

CHAPTER TWENTY-ONE

CORD-YI-GAAAL

After finishing at the hospital, George drove Annie and
Bluey back along the potholed roads to his mum's house.
Turning in between the hedges, the old ute bounced along
the path under an archway of rainforest until it opened up
to gardens, the bungalow, and the big lawn with goal posts
at one end. Mary's great-grand-kids were all playing touch
football.

Boys and girls, ranging in age from fifteen to three
years old, were all zipping and weaving across the green
lawn. Passing and kicking the football, and bumping, laughing and yelling ferociously. All giving as hard as they got,
until Tom-tom, the littlest one with the shock of blond hair,
got the ball.

Then suddenly they all slowed down and faked missing
him. They all dived near but didn't touch him. While the
little fella laughed and beamed and ran – his entire body
wobbling to carry the ball about half his size – all the way
to the try-line.

Everyone yelled, "Put it down! Put it down!" And little Tom-tom bellyflopped down onto the ball and bounced

straight back off it. Both teams cheered and lifted him up on their shoulders to carry him on a victory lap around the field, while Nana Mary cheered.

George collected Tom-tom, his grandson, as he walked past: "Well done, little fella."

"I tried," said Tom-tom.

"Yes, you did," said George. "You scored."

"I tried hard," said Tom-tom.

Annie was walking behind them, and Tom-tom smiled at her over his grandad's shoulder, and said, "See me tried?"

"Yes, I did. You were very good," Annie said, and touched Tom-tom's chubby little fingers hanging off George's shoulder.

Tom-tom asked, "Who's you?"

"Annie."

"She's a friend of Nana Mary's and mine," said George.

Satisfied, Tom-tom turned his head and lay his cheek on George's shoulder. Annie watched him and smiled, and for two seconds forgot her husband's injury. And the hospital bill. And the cow. Then she sneezed.

"Bless oo," said Tom-tom.

"Thanks," said Annie.

"How about a cordial, champ?" asked George.

Tom-tom shouted, "Cord-yi-gaaal!"

"I'll make it," said Annie.

"No, once these savages finish playing footy they'll all want one," said George, "and you'll be in the kitchen for a week."

"Nice place to be," said Annie.

"Nah, just sit here with Mum. I'll look after this rat-bag," said George. He shook Tom-tom off his shoulder and carried him like a football.

Tom-tom yelled to Mary, "I tried!"

Mary smiled at him from her solid, timber, easy chair in the breezeway, then asked Annie, "How's Mitch?"

Annie settled into the chair next to Mary's, and said, "You heard?"

"This is Norfolk Island, dear," said Mary. "No secrets here."

"Not from Mum, anyway," shouted George over his shoulder. "She's the unofficial news station here."

"George, I thought you were making cordial," said Mary.

"Norfolk Island's most trusted source of news and information," said George. "She's like our own CNN. People ring her and tell her the news and she passes it on to her correspondents."

"Sounds like a full-time job," said Annie.

"It doesn't pay much," said Mary. "I can't even get a glass of cordial."

George walked into the house holding Tom-tom, and said, "Nana Mary keeps the island in the know."

"Away with you," said Mary.

Mary and Annie giggled together. Then, after a pause, Mary asked, "So, tell me everything."

Annie relayed everything from Rocco the banded snake eel to the swimming ambos, to the run-in with Roz the receptionist, to the good news about Mitch's likely successful recovery.

In the meantime, the kids had come off the footy ground inundating George with cordial orders. He made sandwiches and drinks and re-settled them all on the far side of the lawn, under the shade of a 90-year-old white oak.

Annie's story had continued throughout the background kerfuffle. She was explaining that Mitch would be in hospital under observation for a day or two, when George returned. He gave Mary and Annie a sandwich and drink and said, "They're going to bill her for the meds."

Mary looked shocked, and said, "Scurrilous. Poor man could've died. And you—young newlyweds—just starting out, watching every cent, no doubt."

Annie dropped her head and said, "Yeah, it's close. I was thinking maybe I could move our flights forward. Go home sooner."

"He can't travel yet, love," said George.

Annie said, "I could—" but then stopped because she couldn't imagine what she could do.

George looked at Mary and said, "Charlie could do with a hand."

Mary looked up at the blue sky and squinted, and hummed a long, quiet, "Hmmm—" as she considered some intergenerational social puzzle.

Annie looked at them quizzically.

George explained to Annie, "Charlie Evans runs a fishing tour around the island, he's flat out."

"The silly season," said Mary.

George asked Annie, "Are you OK on the water?"

"I'm a marine biologist."

"Can you fish?"

Mary said, "She's a marine biologist, George."

George said, "Well, I don't know."

Little Tom-tom dawdled over to them, and Mary asked, "Can you say marine biologist, Tom-tom?"

Tom raised his eyebrows, opened his eyes wide, and said, "Main bludgers."

They all laughed.

Annie said, "Not all of us, Tom-tom."

"Good," said Mary. "That could work. George can call Charlie and say we've got him a deckhand. If that'll help bring in some funds for you?"

Annie looked up at George who nodded. Then she looked at Mary who shone a warm smile that could heat a casserole.

Annie started to say, "Thank you," but her voice caught with emotion. So, she just nodded and smiled, then started crying. Tom-tom waddled over to her and gave her a hug.

CHAPTER TWENTY-TWO

HOSPITAL

Mitch woke groggily from the general anaesthetic with a piercing pain in his groin.

Still semi-conscious, he reached down but hit a tent of blankets where his torso should've been. He felt around but couldn't make sense of the obstruction.

He opened his eyes to the harsh glare of the ward lights and quickly squeezed them shut again, moaning quietly about the pain in his eyeballs. Then he moved his hand and felt up his body for an opening in the blankets. He found the top of the sheet at his neck and manoeuvred his hand under the bedclothes and slid it down his body to investigate the pain in his groin. And when he finally located it, he screamed in agony.

His eyes flew open only to be blasted by the light again. He grimaced and closed them once more, but not before he noticed figures dressed in nurse's uniforms rushing towards him. And like an electric shock, it all came back to him: the eel; the bite; Annie; the water; the love; the wedding; the pool; the cow; the car; the horror ...

PAULO GARNSEY

Mitch squeezed his eyes shut. Tears poured from his slits. He groaned loudly.

Nurse Sarah came to Mitch's side and held his hand. "Are you in pain?"

"Yes."

"On a scale of—"

"Off the bloody scale."

"I'll get the doctor," said the nurse and moved quickly out of the ward. Mitch shook his head to clear the overload of memories and pain. He felt like he was in hell. Attacked from all sides. In his mind, in his body, in his heart, in his soul. The sordid memories drilled into him. The awful pain rose from his most sensitive part. And then, of course, his manhood ... it didn't bear thinking about. Nothing bore thinking about.

Nurse Sarah returned with Dr Pete, who asked, "The pain?"

"Terrible," said Mitch.

"OK, Sarah, let's get him 20 mg of oxycodone for the pain." said Dr Pete, "And while we're waiting, Mitch, is the pain just in the groin?"

"No, everywhere," said Mitch.

"Stomach?"

"Yes," said Mitch.

"The infection may have spread," said Dr Pete. "Let's change the antibiotic infusion to Vancomycin."

"Yes, doctor," said Nurse Sarah.

Nurse Sarah injected the pain relief into the catheter near Mitch's wrist, and said, "Now, count down from 20 to 1."

Mitch counted the numbers quickly in the hope it'd make the drug work faster.

CHAPTER TWENTY-THREE

KNOB

While Mitch was unconscious, Dr Pete and Nurse Sarah removed the tent over his torso and unwrapped the bandages to inspect the wound.

Infection had set in, and Mitch's whole pelvis was inflamed and swollen. So, as well as increasing his painkiller and antibiotics, they replaced his bandages with extra padding to protect Mitch from nudging or pressure.

Later, when he woke, Mitch was feeling no pain. In fact, he was high as a space station. His wound was swollen and heavily bandaged, but distantly throbbing.

He could hear his heartbeat pulsing through his body, and it sounded like an electronic dance song. Mitch started to move his head slightly. It wobbled like a balloon head.

It felt like most of the blood flow was headed to his pelvis, like it was the centre of his body and the rest of him was an appendage hanging off it. He quivered his shoulders slightly and felt like John Travolta in the opening scene of *Saturday Night Fever*. His pulse played the beat of "Stayin' Alive" by the Bee Gees.

The lyrics passed the screen of his mind, and he murmured drunkenly from his bed, "Well, you can tell by the way I use my walk, I'm a woman's man, no time to talk— we're stayin' alive, stayin' alive."

He felt wonderfully disconnected from his body, like his head was on a long bendy pole five metres above his shoulders. He threw back the sheets in time with the beat pulsing through his body. Then, after three attempts, choreographed with his slurred lyrics, "Getting' outta bed, stayin' alive ... Getting' outta bed, stayin' alive," he got out of bed. Sort of.

Mitch was sure he was standing but couldn't feel his feet. It didn't matter, because in his imagination he looked terribly sophisticated. In reality, in Ward One of Norfolk Island Hospital, he was slumped over and mumbling into his hospital gown.

In his imagination, Mitch was in a film clip by Baz Luhrmann. Primary colours were blasting wild action like in *Moulin Rouge*. The nurses were roller skating around the disco floor like Olivia Newton-John in "Xanadu". And he was centre stage – Mitch Travolta, standing there with a monumental penis.

He could look down from his bird's eye view and see his feet, far, far away. But still couldn't feel them. Way down there, on the disco tiles, his feet looked like strange jet-powered shapes from an anime cartoon.

He moved his right foot forwards in a blur of white heelsmoke, then pivoted it backwards to a screech of sound effects. Then he kicked his left foot forwards and backwards in a blur of sparks. He sang, "Feel the city breakin' and everybody shakin', stayin' alive, stayin' alive," in a voice he thought sounded like Beyonce, but was actually more like microphone feedback.

Mitch arched back to hit a particularly high screech and toppled backwards onto his bed. In his imagination, he bounced back off the bed like it was a trampoline. In reality, he muddled in the sheets like a bird tangled in a fishing net.

Then he stood as straight as he could, which took all his concentration because it felt like balancing a long broom in the centre his palm.

Then he felt himself start to spin. Faster and faster, he spun, like a ballet dancer with a massive codpiece doing a pirouette *en pointe*. While around him, on the Hollywood set of a hospital ward, the red and blue lights flashed, and the nurses swooned. And flames rose from where he spun on the tiles, like he was a broomstick spinning in a palm, creating fire.

Mitch reached out and grabbed the hospital IV drip stand and danced with it like Fred Astaire dancing with the hat rack in the famous dance in *Royal Wedding*. Except, in reality, not at all like Fred Astaire.

In reality, Mitch looked like an inebriated tax accountant in a hospital smock under the effects of the maximum safe dose of painkillers.

Unsteadily, he looked down at his faraway bendy body and saw the massive bulge halfway down. "Whoa, boy, whoa!" he said, and pulled at his gown to reveal his bandages: "Why hello there, big boy!"

Nurse Sarah was beside him, saying, "It's alright, Mitch. We used extra bandages. And there's some swelling until the infection dies down."

"Thanks, beautiful," said Mitch, "but I'm a married man now. You missed your chance. Missed your dance."

"Let's get you back to bed," said Nurse Sarah.

"No thanks," said Mitch. "You're lovely, but my wife is lovelier. Where is my wife?"

"She came by earlier," said Nurse Sarah.

Still swaying and semi-naked, he said, "I won't sleep with you, but I'll dance with you."

He tried a dance move with the nurse that he thought was reminiscent of John Travolta and Karen Lynn Gorney on the flashing dance floor of *Saturday Night Fever*. He segued into a strutting Tony Manero solo, with his hands on his hips, and his lips pouting like a serious fish. Then he pointed upwards, towards the four corners of the ceiling, with a lusty rendition of "You should be daaan-ciiing, yehhh."

In Mitch's mind, there were flashing lights under the floor tiles, and crowds were applauding in time as he danced like a svelte anime superstar.

In reality, he looked like a psych patient doing, "I'm a little teapot" then tripping over his own IV drip and falling into Nurse Sarah, who steered him gracefully back to bed.

Nurse Sarah bent over to collect the sheets and pillows from the floor, while Mitch yelled, "Nooo! Wait a minute. Are you—hahaha—are you gonna suck the pus out? Hahaha—Remember that? *Derek and Clive*! Famous!"

Mitch stood back up again, impersonating the drunk comedians, Peter Cook and Dudley Moore in their offensive ranting 1970s show *Derek and Clive*. Admittedly it was better than his impersonation of John Travolta doing Tony Manero, but the content was much worse.

"I've got cancer of the knob," he said, terribly impersonating Dudley Moore's English accent. "Told my wife she has to suck the pus out." Then Mitch fell backwards on the bed laughing, "Hahaha—remember *Derek and Clive*?"

"No, Mitch, but it's OK," said Nurse Sarah, "just get back in—"

Mitch yelled, in a British accent which sounded Jamaican, "Suck the pus out of my knob! Hahaha—"

Mitch laughed uproariously at his awful joke and tried to stand with the assistance of the drip stand, which clattered into a metal tray and crashed to the floor.

"Whoa there!" said Mitch, "Did I do that? Hahaha—"

He saw the upset tray, far away, below him on the disco floor, like he was looking down on it from a tenth-storey window.

"What's happening down there?" Mitch yelled at the tray from his soft-pink, well-insulated penthouse-head, where music was playing and animated birds (similar to the Disney ones) flew around his head, and an audience of colourful fish laughed at his jokes. Then Rocco, the banded snake eel, appeared from behind the bed.

"Hey what are you doing here?" yelled Mitch.

Rocco the (imaginary) banded snake eel said, "I came to see if you're OK."

Mitch said, to an electric cable, "Why thank you! Very kind."

Rocco the (imaginary) banded snake eel said, "No hard feelings?"

Mitch said, to the electric cable, "None at all. You did me a favour. Look at this—" He removed most of his gown and writhed around the ward like the world's worst stripper.

Nurse Sarah shouted, "Mitch, get back to bed, please."

Two more nurses came to help Mitch back to bed.

"No, you can't have me," shouted Mitch as he pushed them away. "I'm married. I love my wife. My wife!"

Dr Pete arrived, calmly pressed the intercom on the wall, and said in his monotone, "Available staff to Ward One."

There weren't any orderlies in the small Norfolk Island Hospital, but within 40 seconds there were four nurses, two doctors, three admin staff, a radiologist, a dental tech, and Bunny, the gardener, putting semi-naked Mitch back into his bed.

"No, no," Mitch yelled. "Rape! Rape—help me, Annie! Annie—"

When they'd restrained him and administered the anaesthetic, he whimpered, "I tried, Annie. I tried to be faithful."

Then he fell asleep.

CHAPTER TWENTY-FOUR

DAMAGES

Nurse Sarah was still cleaning up the ward when Annie arrived to see her husband.

"Oh, no," said Annie.

"Oh yes," said Nurse Sarah, smiling.

She quietly told Annie about the infection and the increase in medication, and how Mitch would have to stay in hospital a few more days.

Annie asked, "He's OK now?"

Nurse Sarah said, "Fine."

Annie asked, "And you?"

"We're all fine," said Nurse Sarah, "just a bit of cleaning up."

"He didn't make this mess, did he?"

"Poor fella," said Nurse Sarah. "He isn't in any pain."

"Oh, no."

"Oh, yes," said Nurse Sarah.

"What happened?"

"He just danced around for a while, proclaiming his love for you. And—" Nurse Sarah squinted trying to remember, then said, "he was quoting something by Dick and Clyde?"

"*Derek and Clive*?"

"That's it!"

"Oh, no!"

"Oh, yes!"

"Not the Greta Garbo skit?"

"No," said Nurse Sarah, "Something about pus—and his knob."

"Oh, no." Annie looked crestfallen.

"Oh, yes."

"The cancerous knob skit," said Annie, "Oh no."

"He's very bandaged down there," Nurse Sarah laughed. "I'm sorry. People do crazy things on analgesics. It was quite funny. Revolting, but funny. We're just lucky there're no other patients."

"Oh, good."

"But he broke some stuff."

"Oh, no."

"Yep."

"Oh well, add it to the bill, I guess," said Annie, "Actually, I'm going out on Charlie Evans's boat. Do you know it?"

"Yep, the *Rainbow Warrior*. I think they're up to number five or six, now. You're doing a fishing tour?"

"Yes. No. I mean, I'm going to work as a deckhand on a fishing tour."

"Oh good. Take your mind off things."

"Yeah. I need to make some money to cover the bills. Or at least pay my way."

"Well don't worry about this," pointing to the broken drip stand. "It's nothing that can't be repaired. We're pretty handy here on Norfolk."

"I'm so sorry."

"It's OK," said Nurse Sarah, "My Uncle Bunny loves fixing things."

Annie looked over at Mitch and said, "I hope everything can be fixed."

"He'll be OK. Give it a few days."

Annie made a sound that could've been the start of crying or laughing. Then she inhaled quickly, and whispered, "Worst honeymoon, ever."

"At least you'll never want to do another one," said Nurse Sarah as she resumed her cleaning.

Annie laughed and said, "Good point. It's definitely my last honeymoon. I just hope we live through it."

Annie moved towards Mitch's bed, leant down and kissed him softly on the lips. She stroked his cheek and said to his unconscious face, "I'm going to get a job on a boat. I'll come back and see you as soon as we dock."

Annie kissed Mitch, again, then left the ward. Both her eyes were filled with tears. She blinked them away, but some streaked down her cheeks. She brushed them away, too, and was smiling by the time she got to George's ute in the car park.

Bluey was sitting on the bench seat next to George, and as Annie opened the door, George said to Bluey, "In the back Blue, make for room for the lady."

"No, it's OK," said Annie. "He can sit next to me."

She patted Bluey and put her arm around him. George drove along the weaving country roads back to Mary's house. At one turn, the fat orange sun was spilling into the sea ahead of them, silhouetting a ridge of Norfolk pines as it went.

George pointed to it and said, "Beautiful sunset."

But Annie didn't see it. She had her eyes closed. And with every turn in the road, she leaned further onto Blue, the dog, and fell deeper asleep. Bluey didn't complain. He just panted with a wide smile.

George told him he was a good dog and drove to his mum's house, where they led Annie up to her bedroom in a trance. She collapsed for 9 hours sleep.

Early the next morning, George collected Annie and they drove back to down to Kingston Pier for a job interview with Charlie Evans, skipper of *Rainbow Warrior VI*.

It was a quick interview.

CHAPTER TWENTY-FIVE

PIER

Norfolk Island's a rare gem in the gleaming Pacific, but it's rough around the edges. High inaccessible cliffs face the ocean on most sides and coral reefs enclose the calm bays on others.

Access by boat is so difficult, French explorer La Perouse said the island was a place for only "angels and eagles to reside" when he failed to land there in 1788.

To provide access, in 1839 the British used convict labour to build a pier from the shore at Kingston out beyond the outer edge of the reef. Today this pier allows the islanders to launch boats out to sea, and to land cargo.

The pier is about as long and as wide as a 100-metre running track. But on either edge, it drops down about three metres to the blue sea. The calm bay on one side, the open ocean on the other. At high tide, waves break over the far end of the pier. In big storms, waves wash along it's whole length.

Halfway along the pier there's a tall yellow crane that's used to lift cargo onto the pier from the small boats. Only these small boats, called lighters, can get over the reef to ferry goods from ships anchored in deeper water.

As well as cargo, the crane also lifts small boats in and out of the water.

George parked his ute at the start of the pier then walked with Annie and Bluey towards the crane, where a large cabin cruiser sat on a trailer hitched to a truck.

The cabin cruiser was under the boom of the crane and a golden man was scaling the boat, attaching the crane-hook to lines from the cabin cruiser. It was not a small boat, but the golden man was climbing over it like a monkey.

The man's curls were cut in a classic Californian beach-bum style, his broad shoulders bulging from the short sleeves of a faded blue polo shirt with "Bounty Fishing Charters" embroidered over the left breast.

Annie marvelled at the athletic ease of the handsome young man. He scarpered over the large boat from aft to bow, and deck to flybridge, completing methodical tasks with heavy equipment. He looked up and noticed George and Annie standing on the pier, and a beaming smile broke across his tanned face. "Uncle!" he shouted and jumped down two metres to land softly on the concrete.

The golden man embraced George and they exchanged greetings in Norfolk. Then he turned his blue eyes onto Annie, and she felt her heart skip a beat. She was afraid she might blush, so she straightened her spine, smiled widely, and met his intense blue eyes.

He lived outdoors, she thought, but obviously smothered himself in SPF 50+ so his face hasn't hardened into a parched desertscape. *Not yet*— she thought, and wondered if he'd still be so beautiful when he was fifty, then she frowned at herself for even wondering it.

They shook hands, smiled at each other, and introduced themselves.

"I'm Charlie Evans, you must be Annie."

"Annie Davidson," then shaking her head, said, "I mean Adams."

"It's OK I forget my name sometimes, too," said Charlie.

"No it's just," said Annie, "I'm just married."

"So I hear," said Charlie, "George tells me you're looking for some work."

"Yep," said Annie.

Charlie asked, "Been on a boat before?"

"Yep," said Annie.

Charlie asked, "Can you bait a hook?"

"Yep," said Annie.

Charlie asked, "When can you start?"

"Now," said Annie.

"Bewdy," said Charlie, "I've got a tour soon. Family of four. Could do with a hand. Should be a few hours. A hundred dollars do ya?"

Annie said, "Make it two hundred."

"Split the diff," said Charlie, "A hundred and fifty."

"Done," said Annie.

They shook hands then turned to George, and, in harmony, said, "Thanks, George."

"Jinx," said Charlie. And they laughed like they'd known each other for years.

George smiled and said, "See youse," and turned back to his ute.

Walking back along the pier, George looked down at Bluey and said, "If I didn't know better, I'd say they'd make a lovely young couple."

Bluey didn't say anything. He just trotted along the wide pier next to George looking ahead to where a compact car was parking too close to the ute. Bluey's ears rose.

George noticed it, too, and said, "What's this arsehole doing?"

Bluey didn't answer. Just frowned at the parking car.

"All this space," said George, "and this arsehole has to park me in."

The passenger door opened against George's work ute and a woman wriggled out of the passenger's side door. Behind her, a teenage girl shimmied out the back seat.

The driver had no trouble getting out of his side of the car. Nor did a young boy in the backseat behind him.

The driver locked the car, put the keys in his pocket, and they all walked along the pier towards the boat.

As he passed them, George said, "Going for a tour?"

Mr Arsehole said, "Pardon me?"

George said, "Going for a fishing tour?"

"Yes," said Mr Arsehole. "Surprisingly expensive. I hope it's worth the money."

George asked, "Where're you from?"

"England," said Mr Arsehole.

George asked, "How much are the deep-sea fishing tours there?"

"Oh—umh, not sure," said Mr Arsehole.

"But it's got the Thames," said Mrs Arsehole.

"Yeah, beautiful," said George. "I bet you miss it."

"Oh, yes," said Mrs Arsehole.

"Ah, well, I'm sure you'll get your money's worth to-day," said George.

"Yes, thank you," said Mrs Arsehole.

And they each walked their own way.

"What did he want, daddy?" asked Hugh.

"Just a local," said Mr Arsehole.

The family made their way to the end of the pier and only twice did the parents feel the need to tell the kids to, "Come away from the edge, or you'll drown."

When the family arrived at the boat, Charlie and Annie peered over the gunwales, down at the pier.

"Ahoy, there!" said Charlie then jumped down to the pier.

Annie, in a clean but old "Bounty Fishing Tours" polo shirt, climbed slowly down to the pier. When she turned around to face the family, Mrs Arsehole gasped at Annie: "What are you doing here?"

Mr Arsehole did a double take and stood with his mouth agape.

Hugh Junior just looked at Annie's breasts pressed against her polo shirt, like he was mesmerised. His sister whispered, "Hugh!" and punched his arm.

Hugh Junior said, "Ouch!"

Charlie said, "You know Annie, my deckhand?"

"Yes," said Mrs Arsehole, "we're acquainted."

"Cool," said Charlie. "Welcome aboard. First things first: safety—"

Charlie went through basic safety training and fitted them all with life jackets.

Then, pointing to the boat on the trailer, Charlie said, "There's two ways to board. You can climb on the boat here.

Then we'll swing it out and lower it into the water. Or you can stay on the pier and step aboard when I lower it level with the pier."

"Which is safer?" asked Mr Arsehole.

"They're both equally safe," said Charlie, "but the first way's more fun."

The kids looked up at their mum expectantly, but she said, "We'll step aboard when it's level with the pier."

"OK," said Charlie. "Let's get underway."

He told the family to move out of the way, then spoke quietly to Annie, "You know her?"

"Yeah, they took our Airbnb and wouldn't let us use the phone," said Annie before adding, "Come to think of it, they did catch us messing around in their pool. So we're probably even."

"Good. I can tell they're pretty tightly wound," said Charlie. "We'll help them to relax. Keep them smiling. OK?"

"You bet," said Annie.

"You get in the truck and follow my instructions," said Charlie, "and we'll hoist the boat, then swing it out. Then we'll lower it a bit, for them to board. Then when they're aboard, you'll lower us all the way into the water, then de-tach the cable, park the truck and jump aboard. OK?"

"Got it," said Annie, wondering if she actually did get it as she walked back to the truck.

Charlie climbed up the side of the cabin cruiser like he was walking up a few stairs. Then he yelled for Annie to drive the truck slowly forwards. The cable attached to the tow bar of the truck's rear bumper became taut, and the lifting straps attached to the boat tightened, and the boat slowly lifted off the trailer.

The Arsehole family watching from the other side of the pier could see that the operation of the crane was a simple pulley system: At one end was the truck; at the other end was the boat; and connecting the two was a cable that ran through the pulley at the top of the crane.

As the truck drove away, the line running through the crane got tight, and the boat was lifted into the air. It was suspended about two metres above the pier when Charlie waved from the boat to the Arsehole family. Only the kids waved back.

"Who wants to push me out?" yelled Charle.

The children raised their hands.

"Ok, push the crane arm out over the water."

They did as they were told and pushed the crane arm towards the side of the pier; the cabin cruiser swung out until it dangled over the water.

"Thanks guys, well done," said Charlie. Then he yelled towards Annie in the truck, "OK, Annie reverse slowly, please."

Annie raised her thumb out the driver's window and put the truck into reverse. As the truck came back towards the crane, the boat slowly descended towards the water.

When it was level with the pier, Charlie yelled, "Stop there, Annie."

The truck stopped and the boat hung in mid-air a few metres above the water. Charlie bounced two fenders over the gunwales to cushion the boat against the pier, and yelled to Annie, "Pull the brake on, Annie, and help the crew aboard."

A few seconds later Annie got out of the truck and said to the family "OK, let's get aboard."

The family picked up their day packs, hats, phones, and water bottles. Then followed Annie to where the pier met the boat.

"Be careful here," said Annie. "Hold onto the railing as you step across."

The family and Annie stood on the pier, while Charlie stood on the dangling boat. The gap between them was about one foot.

Charlie stepped one foot on to the pier, and bridged the gap, and held out a hand to the family, saying, "Who's first?"

They all looked at Mr Arsehole, who nodded, "I'll go."

"Hold my arm and step aboard, sailor," said Charlie.

He did it easily.

Next was the young girl. "Well done, little lady," said Charlie. She blushed.

Then Hugh Junior jumped aboard, slipped, and landed on his bum. He shrieked and looked like he was about to cry but Charlie bent down quickly and lifted him up, saying, "Nice landing, sailor. Lucky you landed on your butt-cakes. Eh?"

Hugh Junior giggled as a tear ran down his cheek, and Charlie whispered to him, "Don't let Mrs Annie see you cry."

Hugh looked over at Annie, and her polo shirt. And wiped his cheek with the back of his hand.

"Right to go, sailor?"

"Uh huh," Hugh nodded.

"Yes, skipper?"

"Yes, skipper," said Hugh.

"That's more like it," said Charlie.

He placed the boy safely back on deck, then turned his charm on Mrs Arsehole, saying, "Now don't you try that one, darling. I wouldn't want to see you damage that fine hiney." Then he smiled like a talk show host as he held out his hand to her.

Her mouth opened to complain but her eyebrows wavered, then her eyes shone with a distant fire. She shook her head and made a sound like a shy horse. Then she dropped her head and held her hand out for Charlie as she stepped elegantly, but quickly aboard.

"Great work everyone," said Charlie. "Now go and reverse us into the water please, Annie."

Annie went back to the truck and reversed it slowly, until the boat touched the water, and she heard Charlie yell, "OK. That's it."

Then Charlie lowered the twin Evinrudes into the water and started them up. Then he detached the crane hook from the harnesses aboard the *Rainbow Warrior VI,* and shouted, "Drive forward, Annie."

Annie moved the truck forwards to raise the empty hook up from the water. She unhitched the cable from the tow bar of the truck and parked the vehicle, then ran back along the pier. She walked carefully down the slippery concrete steps to water level just as Charlie bought the boat alongside.

Annie stepped aboard and Charlie steered *Rainbow Warrior VI* away from the pier, and yelled, "Let's hunt us some fishies."

Charlie pointed at the waves crashing on the reef ahead and said, "There's gaps in the reef there," he pointed, "And there. We'll wait and time our run between waves." Then he eased the throttle back and said, "Wait—"

"Wait—"

The kids nudged each other to get a better view but Mrs Arsehole scolded them with a look.

"Wait—" said Charlie.

"Go!" and Charlie gently pushed the throttle forward and slid through the gap on a buffer of backwash.

Looking ahead at the larger swells outside the reef, Charlie said, "That'll probably be the most exciting part of the trip, I'm afraid. But we'll do it again on the way back."

"Now," said Charlie turning to face the family, "everyone sit back and relax and the lovely Mrs Annie will serve you cold drinks."

Annie handed out wine under the distasteful lashes of some, and soft drinks under the loving glances of others, smiling at all.

The boat was on the high water now. The twin outboards churning smoothly through choppy conditions. The passengers were all sipping their drinks and looking out to sea, so Annie went into the wheelhouse with Charlie.

Hugh Junior watched her go, and said to his mother, "Are they trespassing?"

"What are you talking about, Hugh Junior?"

"Ummhhh," said Hugh.

"Look! An island," said Brooklyn, pointing at Phillip Island as a diversion.

In the wheelhouse Annie said to Charlie, "A question, skipper."

"Sure, deckie."

"With the pier and the crane," said Annie, "wouldn't it be easier—"

Charlie held up a hand to stop her, then said, "You're not going to tell me about your idea to extend the pier out another hundred metres, are you? Or to motorise the crane? Or to use drones to bring in the cargo? Or deepen the channel to bring the ships in closer?"

Annie's mouth opened but before she could answer, Charlie continued, "I get it from tourists every day. 'Why don't you build a pier?' they say. And I feel like saying, 'Why don't *you* build a fuckin' pier?' Think we've never thought of it? In over 160 years? They're here two days and think they've got it sussed."

Charlie looked at Annie whose mouth was now closed as she listened to him continue, "This is one of the oldest ports in Australia," he said. "We've tried everything. A harbour pier will cost millions. Australia already owns us over a $13 million debt for resurfacing the international airport. Who'll own us for hundreds of millions? The Chinese?"

Annie said quietly, "I wasn't going to say that."

"Ok, sorry," said Charlie. "A bit touchy. Everyone has an idea about how to improve the shipping, but most of them have no idea. They haven't even seen it when it's rough."

"No," said Annie. "I've got an idea for catching fish without a boat."

"Eh?"

"The cleanest ocean water in the world's right here, right?" said Annie pointing to the deep blue sea all around them.

"Yep."

"Why not use it for an aquaculture operation?"

"Fishing without a boat," said Charlie, "now that's a good suggestion."

"Best ocean water in the world is at your doorstep," said Annie, "just pump it into the facility."

Charlie said, "Build the fish farm on land or at sea?"

"On land is easier to control," said Annie, "but build it right next to the ocean. And you'd still grow fish that are native to this area."

Charlie said, "Trumpeter?"

"Perfect," said Annie, "Fly them direct from the airport to Sydney and Brisbane markets."

"You know about this stuff, how?"

"I'm a marine biologist," said Annie. "Worked on aquaculture operations all over the world. Cairns, Melbourne, PNG, China, Europe. Set up fish farms from Hong Kong to Saudi Arabia. And this is the best water I've ever seen."

"It's a good idea," said Charlie. "Personally, I like fishing with tourists—when they're not telling me how to fix the pier—but I can't even keep up with the demand for fish from the local restaurants, here, on Norfolk. With aquaculture, we could export."

CHAPTER TWENTY-SIX

SCURRILOUS

Norfolk Island Radio operates from a small timber building under an enormous antenna, in the middle of a wide green paddock lazy with cows.

Inside the studio, wearing headphones and sitting in front of their microphones, are the announcers for this show: Father Pat and Mr Music, DJ Ken.

It's the weekly Rock 'n' Roll 'n' Rugby Radio Show, as it is every Thursday at 3 pm. But unlike normal weeks, when they'd be talking about football or music, Father Pat has abandoned the usual format for a "lost and found" announcement.

Father Pat: I gotta tell you, Kenny, it's too good. You'll hear about it on the usual Norfolk Island channels, if you haven't already.

DJ Ken: *Dem tell*? (Gossip?)

Father Pat: Yep. But I wanted to tell you first. The real story.

DJ Ken: I thought it was a lost and found announcement.

Father Pat: It is. But that's just the start of it. This one's got everything. Love. Loss. Violence. Infidelity. Even the knob scene from *Derek and Clive*.

DJ Ken: Who?

Father Pat: Before your time, Young Ken. Which is lucky because it's too blue for the censorship laws of this radio station. Any radio station! It even made the nurses blush in Ward One.

DJ Ken: And they've heard it all.

Father Pat: Oh, yeah, stalwart breed, the nurse, that's for sure.

DJ Ken: Right up there with coppers, teachers and soldiers.

Father Pat: And ambos. And they're in this story, too.

DJ Ken: OK, Father Pat, you've whet my appetite. Who's this *Derek and Clive*?

Father Pat: I'll start with the lost and found announcement.

DJ Ken: Go for it, father.

Father Pat: It's a gold wedding ring. And it must be one of the more amazing stories to happen in Norfolk since—

DJ Ken: There's been a few.

Father Pat: Since author, Colleen McCullough?

DJ Ken: Or since the singer, Helen Reddy, lived here?

Father Pat: Or since the story of the Bloody Bridge.

DJ Ken: How about the mutineers? Gotta be the best story ever.

Father Pat: Gotta be.

DJ Ken: Or Barney Duffy, the convict who evaded capture by living in the hollow of a tree trunk for seven years!

Father Pat: Oh, yeah, Norfolk Island has her fair share of howlers. And this one is the best one since—Well, at least the best one this week.

DJ Ken: So far.

They started giggling. And this would underscore the rest of the radio show.

Father Pat: Yes, so far. So buckle-up, children, and wrap your ears around this yarn. It starts with a gold wedding ring, which I have in my right hand, right now. And it's inscribed—I'm reading on the inside of the ring here—"Annie, Love Eternal, Mitch".

In Ward One, Mitch heard the voices, lifted his head slowly from the pillow, and looked towards the small radio on a ledge near the door.

Below deck of the *Rainbow Warrior VI*, which was anchored about 60 kilometres from Norfolk Island, Annie was swaying from side to side in the galley while cutting up sandwiches for the guests who were hanging lines over the sides of the boat. She suddenly stopped mid-slice and looked at the small radio speakers inset into the marine ply panel.

Meanwhile, in the studio, DJ Ken and Father Pat continued their banter.

DJ Ken: You know them?

Father Pat: Well if my guess is right, it's the couple who arrived for their honeymoon last flight—

DJ Ken: Yesterday?

Father Pat: Nope, day before. But since then—cop this: I picked them up at the airport. Gave them their rental. Within eight minutes—the shortest insurance claim I've seen—they ran into a cow. One of George and Smiley's.

DJ Ken: Oh yeah, I heard about this. This was Mildred, yes?

On a tractor, in a paddock, Bluey, the dog, was sitting next to George who was driving between rows. They both suddenly looked at the small transistor radio hanging from the canopy. The tractor stopped.

In the office of the hardware store, George's wife, Smiley, was calculating a row of figures. Suddenly she stopped writing and looked at the radio on the shelf. Sadness teared up her eyes, and she dropped her head and held her forehead.

In the canteen of Norfolk Island School, George and Smiley's daughter Polly was sitting at a table with her friends. They all suddenly looked at the speakers playing the radio show. Polly cried and dropped her head into her hands in a gesture that mirrored her mum's, and her friends from all the tables came over to comfort her.

Meanwhile, back in the little studio under the enormous antenna . . .

Father Pat: Mildred is still with the vet, and we don't know if she'll pull through. But the car's definitely deceased. Our honeymooners were worse for wear but fortunately OK. Then these two—

DJ Ken: It goes on?

Father Pat: It's hardly started, my friend.

DJ Ken: Get a cuppa.

Father Pat: And a bottle.

They both giggled.

Father Pat: Then they find their Airbnb is double booked.

On the deck of the *Rainbow Warrior VI*, Mr and Mrs Arsehole and Brooklyn and Hugh Junior, all look towards the speakers on the wheelhouse. The kids looked to their parents for a reaction, who just turned their heads back to the fishing lines. So Brooklyn and Hugh Junior did the same.

Back in the studio, under the headphones ...

DJ Ken: Silly season.

Father Pat: That's it, Ken, silly season. So, day one of their honeymoon: no car, no place to stay, accumulated debt for damages to livestock and automobiles, already in the thousands.

DJ Ken: Poor *sullen*.(People)

Father Pat: But then grace shines upon them—in the form of our Lady Saint of Norfolk Island. Mother Mary takes them in.

On her knees, in her garden, Mary Christian-Bailey was weeding around her roses. She didn't even look towards the 1974 transistor radio babbling away at her side. She just said, "Oh get away with you, Patrick Crenshaw. Always were a scallywag."

Back in the little studio under the huge antenna in the paddock of cows ...

DJ Ken: I assume you're talking about Mary Christian-Bailey, here?

Father Pat: One and the same.

DJ Ken: Gives them a place to stay after they ran over her son's cow?

Father Pat: Yep.

DJ Ken: She's a saint.

Father Pat: Took in the weary travellers when all the lodges were full.

DJ Ken: Don't tell me they had an immaculate conception?

Father Pat: Well, immaculate might be the only chance of conception because—

DJ Ken: Wait. What?

Then DJ Ken and Father Pat started laughing.

Father Pat: No—Wait—Stop. Listen. They went to Emily Bay and lost their ring.

DJ Ken: This ring?!

In Ward One, Mitch moved uncomfortably in his bed so he could squint directly at the radio. The nurses diplomatically found other things to do.

In the galley of *Rainbow Warrior VI*, Annie held the knife in her hand and leaned her head towards the speaker and squinted to hear better.

In the headphones in the studio, Father Pat said, "This ring, here."

DJ Ken: No!

Father Pat: Yep. But wait, it gets better.

DJ Ken: No!

Father Pat: Yep.

Father Pat: While trying to find this ring here—That's why I've chosen the next song, "Return the Ring" by The Smiths.

DJ Ken: Only Morrissey could cover such pathos.

Father Pat: Yes. But wait—While looking for it, deep in Emily Bay, Mitch gets bitten on the old fella.

In Bed Two of Ward One, Mitch stared . . .

In the galley, on *Rainbow Warrior VI*, Annie stared . . .

In the tractor, on the farm, Bluey and George stared . . .

In the office, at her desk, Smiley stared . . .

In the canteen, at the high school, Polly and her friends stared . . .

In her garden, on her knees, Mary stared . . .

In every place on Norfolk Island, everyone stared . . .

. . . at their radios.

And there was dead air.

In the middle of the Pacific Ocean, in the middle of Norfolk Island, in the middle of a green paddock lazy with cows, in the small building with an enormous antenna, DJ Ken stared at Father Pat with his mouth dropped open, and there was dead air for a few seconds. Then Ken exhaled like he was deflating and said quietly into his microphone, "Nooooo—"

Father Pat: Yep.

DJ Ken: No-oooo!

Father Pat: Yes-sss.

DJ Ken: *That* guy!

Father Pat: *That* guy.

In bed, in hospital, Mitch screamed. Nurse Sarah came quickly to his side. She pressed the buzzer for assistance.

In the studio, DJ Ken said, "But I heard his missus bit it off."

In the galley, on the boat, Annie screamed. Charlie came in from the deck and put his hand on her shoulder. Annie turned to him and fell into his muscled shoulder. And she sobbed tears onto his faded polo shirt. Charlie put his arms around and hugged her.

In the studio in the paddock, DJ Ken was still going: "I heard it was because she caught him cheating with Roz, the receptionist."

At the reception desk, in the hospital, Roz screamed. Her colleagues all looked at her and Roz turned to them and shook her head and said, "No—No—No!"

In the studio, under the antenna, Father Pat said, "No—no—no. Not true. But the true story is even better."

In Ward One of Norfolk Island's Hospital, Dr Pete walked quickly through the door and saw Nurse Sarah struggling to restrain Mitch who was wrestling to get out of his bed. Dr Pete calmly pressed the intercom: "Available staff to Ward One."

In Studio One of Norfolk Island Radio, DJ Ken said, "What could be better than that?"

Father Pat: An eel.

DJ Ken: A what?

Father Pat: A banded snake eel.

DJ Ken laughed so hard his head jolted backwards and his headphones fell off. When he'd collected himself, he said, "I'm sorry, sorry, what? A banded snake eel bit the honeymooner's knob off?"

In Ward One, Dr Pete and Nurse Sarah were joined by three nurses, a dental technician and Bunny, the gardener, to restrain Mitch. Dr Pete held Mitch's arm, near the canula, and said to Nurse Sarah, "Sarah, let's get him ten mils of Midazolam."

When she was gone, Dr Pete said, "And someone, please turn that stupid radio off."

On the boat, Annie cried and Charlie reached over her shoulder and turned the radio off.

In the radio station, they were laughing too much to say anything except segments of words.

Father Pat: Not off. Just a bit—

Before descending into laughter.

DJ Ken inhaled noisily.

DJ Ken: It bit—a bit?

Father Pat was laughing so much he slipped from his chair. Which made DJ Ken laugh even harder. In between gasps, he said, "Want—a tip? Don't—swim—with—an—eel," Before prolonged laughter and two words, "S-s-song—R-r-ring—"

DJ Ken pressed the button on the third attempt and played the song, "Return the Ring" by The Smiths.

In her garden, Mary was still wearing her gardening gloves as she held the phone. Her sweet face was flushed, and her voice was agitated as she muttered, "Scurrilous."

In her office at the hardware store, Smiley held the phone with one hand, and her forehead with the other. Her cute face was wet with tears, as she said, "Scurrilous."

CHAPTER TWENTY-SEVEN

RADIO

In the studio, after the song, the two announcers had regained their composure.

DJ Ken: Great band.

Father Pat: Of a time. They introduced the whole "shoe gazing" thing.

DJ Ken: And dancing like you're ice skating.

Father Pat: Took Emo out of the dark.

DJ Ken: New Order meets The Cure. But better lyrics than both.

Father Pat: And that's what I'll be doing straight after the show.

DJ Ken: Ice skating?

Father Pat: No. Returning the ring. Take it up to Mitch in the hospital. Can't take it to Annie, the wife. She's out on Charlie's boat.

DJ Ken: *Rainbow Warrior*?

Father Pat: Yep. Working. Paying off the debts.

All around the island, people were glued to their radio. Some crying, some laughing, some shaking their heads, some nodding. Some clenching their fists. Some holding their foreheads. All listening to the only radio station in town.

In the studio ...

Father Pat: Used all their honeymoon money to pay for the car and the hospital.

DJ Ken: Worst honeymoon. Ever.

Father Pat: Well, yes, and no.

DJ Ken: What do you mean, Father Pat?

Father Pat: That's what the next song is about, Ken.

DJ Ken: Bob Dylan's, "Hard Rain". But the Bryan Ferry version.

Father Pat: Yes, because they've had some hard rain, these honeymooners. No doubt about it. But here, on Norfolk Island, we know rain. It makes the grass green. And the cows fat and happy. And the pine trees strong and flexible. And the people resilient.

DJ Ken: It also makes floods and landslides.

Father Pat: And it could go either way for this couple.

DJ Ken: We'll see.

Father Pat: Stay tuned.

CHAPTER TWENTY-EIGHT

ESCAPEE

When Mitch woke from his sedative, his face was crumpled with sleep and worry. He grimaced as he gazed around the ward to get his bearings. When he saw the radio on the ledge, his face went red with anger and shame. He looked to the young nurse sitting near the end of his bed, and said, "Where's the radio station?"

The young nurse, said, "The radio station? Why? Oh!" Then she realised why he was asking. "Oh, don't worry about Father Pat. He's just trying to get the facts straight."

Mitch threw off his sheets and moved out of bed as quickly as his injury would allow. Which was, in fact, very slowly.

So slowly, the young nurse didn't even notice until Mitch was almost at the door. Then she said, "Hey, where are you going?"

Mitch didn't answer. The nurse followed him to the hospital exit door, badgering him with information like, "You aren't supposed to be moving", and "The doctor may not like it".

But none of it distracted Mitch's departure through the hospital doors, so she changed tack and said, "It's lunch soon. Don't go far."

Then she watched as he turned the corner of the building. "Poor bugger," she said, clicking her tongue as she closed the door and went inside to tell Nurse Sarah.

Mitch rounded the corner, stopped, and leaned hard against the building. He closed his eyes and inhaled through clenched teeth at the pain from his groin. Then he dropped his head and bent slightly and exhaled, "Oh fuck," through the grill of his teeth.

Bent over like that, tears dripped out of his eyes and fell onto his bare feet on the lush green grass.

First, it was about the pain. Then, the shame. Then, the utter desperation. And finally, as he leaned against the weatherboard hospital, Mitch sobbed in self-pity about the tragic events that'd wrenched him from his beloved.

CHAPTER TWENTY-NINE

MAISIE

After his radio show, Father Pat left the studio and turned on his phone. There were many dings, from many messages, but the only one he opened was from "Daa Randa".

He read it and bowed his head. Tears flooded his eyes as he leaned against the timber wall of the small building under the enormous antenna, in the middle of the vast green paddock.

A black and white cow with wide brown eyes looked up from the green grass it was chewing to stare at Father Pat. Father Pat shook his head at the cow, and said, "What are you looking at?"

The cow didn't say anything but lowered its head to chomp more grass. Father Pat smiled with sad green eyes. Then he inhaled deeply and walked through the paddock on the short-cut to the back of the hospital.

When he arrived at Daa Randa, Father Pat consoled Terry, the wardsman. Then he held the hands of two crying nurses, Jane and Lill, and nodded as they told him how much they loved Maisie Buffett.

He nodded and smiled as they told stories through gulping tears of the delightful things Maisie had done. How much they loved her. How, even though she'd been silent for a decade, she had shone. She'd radiated a light all her days, even her last. How she was tiny and gentle like a white tern, who flitted lightly around the home, bringing joy to everyone who'd lived, worked, and visited there.

Father Pat remembered Maisie from his earliest childhood. He remembered the gallery of faces he'd seen pass through since then and felt like his ribs would burst from the grief. But he smiled with Jane and Lill, and squeezed their hands, and nodded knowingly.

He didn't know what he was supposed to know, but he knew grief. He knew, like Dylan and Ferry, a hard rain is gonna fall. So you best carry an umbrella of faith.

He asked Jane and Lill to gather the other staff so they could all say the last rites over Maisie's body.

Then he went to the next room to ask Maisie's best friend, Alice Young, if she wanted to say goodbye too.

Alice didn't stop staring out the windows at the moving trees. "Fuck her! She left me without saying goodbye. I ain't gonna say bye to her, neither."

And she locked her old jaw muscles tight to retain the dam of tears built up behind.

Father Pat nodded and smiled and felt the fire of love burning fiercely in his heart. He knew Alice just wanted to go with her friend.

"All right, my lovely," he said, "I'll see you tomorrow."

"Bring us some bungers, will ya?" said Alice. "I think I'll take up smoking, again."

"Didn't know you'd given up," said Father Pat.

"Yeah, did it for Maisie," said Alice. "She wanted me to be healthy. Well fuck that."

The dam burst. Alice started to cry. Father Pat moved quickly to her side and kneeled next to her chair. She leaned into him, and he put his arms around her tiny, sobbing shoulders as she bawled into his shirt.

Father Pat whispered, "God, look after our beautiful mate, Maisie. She did you proud."

"And look after us, too," said Alice. "We're giving our best down here."

Soon, the nurse brought Alice a cup of tea with a shot of rum. Then Father Pat went into Maisie's room and stood next to the head of the bed, where her frail little body was outlined under a white sheet. He said the last rites as the nurses, Jane and Lill, and the receptionist, Evie, and the bookkeeper, Les, all cried. Terry, the wardsman, stood at the end of the bed with his fingers resting gently on the sheet where it rose over Maisie's toes.

CHAPTER THIRTY

DANCE

Father Pat left Daa Randa and walked along the path towards the car park. He was looking down at the lush green
grass beside the path, wondering about this brief, wondrous,
heartbreaking life we have.

This spark. This cycle. This rich, impossible glistening
tedious magic. This rapture. This bag of blood and bones
we wear, dancing on a spinning blue ball in space, for
decades if we're incredibly lucky. Or unlucky. He wasn't
sure sometimes.

Pat wondered how we all didn't simply explode with
the amazement of it all. Deep in his thoughts, he stepped
onto the grass just so he could feel its spongey sumptuous-
ness under his Hush Puppies.

Mitch noticed the movement to his left. Saw it was the
priest.

All that sorrow and self-pity, all the shame and pain and
mournful longing, all of it suddenly galvanised into a steel
fist rising from Mitch's guts. It bubbled into blind fury on
its way past his burning heart, then exploded from his throat

in a war cry, "Aaa-aaa-argh," as his bare feet sprinted across the spongey green grass.

The Hush Puppies stopped.

Mitch's pyjama-ed legs were a blur as his bare feet ran across the lawn towards them.

Father Pat's first reflex was to slide his right Hush Puppy backwards and angle his left one inwards, into the boxing stance he'd learnt at the seminary. His second thought was one of compassion for a person who was suffering. Pat's fists unclenched. He dropped his hands and opened his palms towards Mitch. And that was how he took the first punch.

Mitch screaming. Pat reeling. Mitch a wild beast. Pat a staggering fool. The rain started falling.

Mitch clung to the older man's back and rode him like a drunk on a hog. All physical pain was lost in the red–black rage. Pat fended off the blows that rained down to either side of his head, as they piggy-backed around the lush green courtyard.

Pat suddenly buckled his legs, jolted his shoulders, and flicked Mitch onto the grass. The madman in pyjamas rose up, screaming in fury before Pat had even managed to stand upright.

Mitch was on him again. And the rain was falling. And they were dancing face to face in a punk dervish of blows, and nails, and butts, and knees.

Four staggering feet – two shod, two bare – tripping to stay upright on the wet green grass.

Their red faces pressed against each other. Mitch screaming incoherence, Pat wincing from the spittle, and contorting with the effort of compassion. Then, suddenly, changing; Pat was screaming back at Mitch, "Stop! Stop! Stop it! Stop!"

Then he pushed Mitch away and flicked his fists up into a fighting pose.

"Wait! Wait!" said Pat.

"No!"

"Wait!" he repeated.

"Aaaaargh!" Mitch lowered his head and started running forwards again.

Father Pat yelled, "Want me to kick your dick?"

Mitch slowed and widened his eyes.

Father Pat said, "That's all I gotta do."

Mitch stopped moving. Rain fell harder.

"Then it's permanent. Back in surgery," said Father Pat.

Mitch roared heaving breaths from his wild red face.

"Lose your dick?" yelled Pat. "Want that?"

The rain splashed on them, but both were fixed to their spots.

Mitch yelled, "You fucking fuckwit. You fucking cunt. You said that shit on the fuckin' radio for everyone to hear."

Father Pat yelled back, "They already knew. And worse. Terrible rumours. That's how it works here. You gotta get the facts out as soon as possible."

"Facts?!" Mitch yelled, "How about the fact my life's ruined? Over! Marriage—over! My cock—" He bent in pain then straightens himself, "—bad. My wife, whom I love—" as his tears join the rain "—like you love Jesus, is out on some boat with some male model, some Don Juan bastard, and you're making fun—"

"What *are* you talking about?" said Pat. "Are you mad?"

By now the usual suspects had arrived to watch the drama. Doctors, nurses, admin ladies (excluding Roz), the psychologist, the dentist, the dental assistant, three gardeners, a plumber who was there to fix the staff toilets, and eight hospital visitors, all standing under the covered walkway and the eaves of the hospital building as the rain fell on the fighters.

Yesterday, they saw the wife attack Roz the receptionist. Then some saw this guy dancing naked during his hallucinatory escapade. Now, they'd just seen him punch the priest.

Many were thinking, "What's this crazy man up to now?"

Others, who'd seen him at his worst and heard the full story on the radio, now had compassion. He was no longer just another crazy tourist passing through their world. They'd seen this guy warts and all. The ones who knew what life on the island could throw at you, felt a streak of admiration that he wasn't taking it lying down.

A few were even touched by the way he spoke about his wife – despite the profanity and the woman's obvious foibles. And they all knew the priest, Father Pat. Many were related to him. They knew he had a good heart even if he had unorthodox methods.

So, no one was butting in. And no one was jeering them on. They were all just standing in clumps of two or three around the fighters, letting them sort it out. Feeling the pain as it went.

"What are ya' talkin' about?" yelled Pat.

"The fuckin' fisherman," yelled Mitch.

"What fuckin' fisherman?" yelled Pat.

"Fuck you!" yelled Mitch and started moving forward again.

"The one who caught your ring?" Father Pat pulled it from his pocket.

Mitch stopped.

"Caught it in a kingfish's tail. Let that sink in. Caught it in a fuckin' fish! Handed it in to the radio station," said Pat, "That's why I came here, to see if it's yours."

Father Pat was holding it in his palm. It looked nothing like the ring Mitch had given Annie two days ago. It was a ring of teeth clenched around a band of gold. It looked like a heavy-metal biker ring.

"You idiot," laughed Mitch, "That's not Annie's."

Father Pat looked at it again, and moved it around his hand, then held it closer and squinted, "But it has your names inscribed."

"Bullshit," said Mitch and thrust out his palm, "Give us a look."

As soon as it landed in his palm, he knew by its exact weight that it was Annie's. Knew it internally, on a scale somewhere near his heart.

His mouth opened when he saw the inscription. His head dropped and his knees buckled, and he fell to the wet green grass. A moan of grief pumped up from a deep bend in his lower intestine.

The nurses were first to him. Then the gardeners and the plumber, then the dentist and psychologist. They all crowded around, reached out their hands and lifted him up, saying things like, "It's alright, mate," and, "We got you."

Nurse Sarah went over to Father Pat, and said, "Here, let me have a look at you." She tilted his head back and said, "He got you a good one, there."

"Lucky shot," said Father Pat. "Caught me unawares."

Nurse Sarah laughed and said, "Come on Muhammad Ali, we'll get you cleaned up inside."

Then to the others, she said, "Come on, *yorli*. It's not a petting zoo. Get Mike Tyson inside."

CHAPTER THIRTY-ONE

WEATHER GIRL

You'd think any job with "marine" in the title would provide useful experience on the ocean. But when the attached noun is "biologist", they generally can't help you much in a storm. They're trained to tell you what's living in the water. Not what's getting blown to bits in a boat on top of it.

Fortunately, Annie got into the marine part of biology from the desert region of Western Queensland, where weather is everything.

Windorah. One of the driest places on the driest continent on Earth.

Growing up there, Annie Davidson didn't see rain until she was eight years old. When it did come, it was heaven on Earth. The most valuable resource in her world, literally, raining down freely from the sky.

Her parents danced in it. Her nana danced in it. Her brothers and sisters danced in it. All whooped with joy in a scene that far outstripped all the Christmas dances put together.

The soil reacted instantly, sending the new smell of petrichor into the air everywhere.

Within hours, grass shoots sprung out of the red ground.

Within days, new flowers grew.

Within a week, inland lakes formed. The red earth liquified into vast seas.

Then, the exotic birds arrived: pelicans, spoonbills, ibises, egrets. The skies went white with cockatoos, grey with herons, purple with swamphens.

Best of all, the dry creek beds – which Annie had only known as barren gullies – suddenly flowed with megalitres of the magic stuff.

And what did that bring?

Fish!

She insisted on accompanying her father and brothers to the flowing creeks. They were surprised at the patience of this young girl with a fishing line in her hand, who lured more than her fair share of barramundi, bream, perch, and mangrove jack.

She was told to be careful near the water's edge, because the creeks could rise quickly and pull a child down. She heeded the advice and respected the magic liquid when she waded in the shallows to catch new water insects in her hands.

With a net Annie caught reptiles and amphibians and popped them in a jar. At home, she researched them in the family's *Encyclopedia Britannica* and noted them down in the columns of her Spirax notebook.

INSECTS	NO.	CRUSTACEANS	NO.	AMPHIBIANS	NO.	FISH	NO.
Blue Skimmer	12	Common Yabbie (Cherax Destructor)	3	Barking Frog	1	Bream	5
				Bumpy Rocketfrog	1	Mangrove Jack	8
				Chubby Gungan	1	Perch	4

Within a month, the rain had stopped.

Within a season, the land had hardened, again. The faces of the people had hardened again, too.

Annie wondered where it'd gone. She asked her parents and teachers, but none provided adequate answers. And this bright, little, mystified girl followed the miracle and mystery of rain into a lifetime of studying the weather.

She thought if she could learn enough, she could bring the rain back. But the rain didn't return to Windorah for another eight years.

The rivers dried. The grass died. The stock starved. Annie's parents slaved.

In this torture, Annie studied the intricacies of weather, but nothing could break the drought. Not study, not prayer, not even rain dances under a billion lonely stars.

Annie recorded the Southern Oscillation Index every morning for seven years.

Then, on 17 April 2012, when Annie was fifteen years old, she noted the equatorial trade winds becoming stronger. After her years of study, she made an educated guess that a change was coming.

Annie begged her parents to hold out for one more season. She begged her parents to beg the banks to hold out for one more season. She said there were weather indications of an impending La Niña weather event that'd bring the rain back. It'd save the stock. It'd bring a smile back to her father's face. It'd bring heaven back to Earth.

No one took the teenage girl seriously. The banks knew the price of cheap land. When they foreclosed on the family property Annie took it as a personal failure.

After four generations there, the Davidsons left their home in Windorah forever. They drove 1,300 kilometres east to the coast. Her nana didn't make the trip. Her father may as well not have.

Annie's mum worked in hotels in Surfers Paradise. The boys followed the work, far away, to mines in Mount Isa and Western Australia.

Annie witnessed her entire family disappear over a matter of months. Then one night, she watched news reports of rain falling in the channel country and in Windorah. That moment galvanised Annie's lifelong love of science, and her hatred of banks.

She refused to ever enter a bank again. Let alone trust them with a cent of her money. Or God forbid, go into their debt!

Instead, she entered Griffith University on a scholarship and studied the science of water. Hydrology, meteorology, and eventually her master's in marine biology – up at James Cook university in Townsville.

So, you'd think this particular marine biologist would be a handy person to have aboard a boat during a storm. But Annie knew – better than anyone – no matter how much you study, sometimes there's nothing you can do.

When a storm's sweeping the ocean, shifting the sea, and spinning the boat, it doesn't matter what noun you have aboard. The only word that matters is "mariner". And that described Charlie.

The best Annie could do was ensure Charlie knew which way the cyclone was coming and advise full speed the other way. Fortunately, that direction was west, back towards Norfolk Island.

She could pray they made it back in time. But after the week she'd had, Annie wasn't brimming with confidence.

Fortunately, Charlie Evans was a born mariner. His parents ran Norfolk Fishing Tours and Charlie was raised aboard their boats. His grandfather was a whaler. His grandmother, one of the wives who'd stood on the cliffs out at Anson Bay on cloudy nights when their men were at sea, singing their song to the waves so their sailor men could hear their voices and know which direction was home.

Charlie knew the ocean around Norfolk Island better than almost anyone, but he had a fight on his hands with this storm.

The Arsehole family also had a fight on their hands. Their fight was with seasickness. All four were losing badly.

CHAPTER THIRTY-TWO

HOSPITAL

Depending on your beliefs, a priest may also be a useful person to have around during a storm. But Father Pat wasn't proving useful to Mitch.

The two of them occupied neighbouring beds in Ward One. Separated by a plastic hospital curtain, Nurse Sarah tended to Father Pat's injuries, while Dr Pete and the two other nurses worked on Mitch.

Mitch's bandages were off, and a nurse was cleaning the wound with a bottle of saline and a swab in a scissor-clamp. Mitch was trying not to notice. He stared hard at the perforated, white ceiling tiles.

Dr Pete was pressing into soft areas around Mitch's belly and pelvis, saying, "Does that hurt?" and "How about there?"

Mitch was shaking his head, but really just to clear his mind and take his attention from what the nurse was doing.

On the other side of the curtain, Nurse Sarah dabbed at the purple lump under Father Pat's left eye, and said quietly, "Got you a good 'un, Pat."

"He king hit me," said Father Pat.

Mitch heard and piped up, "Next time I'll warn you, old man. Like this: 'I'm going to hit you as soon as I stand up.' How's that?"

Nurse Lucy put her hand on his head and said, "Shhhh," and eased his head back to the pillow.

Father Pat retorted, "I turned the other cheek, last time, boy-o. Next time you won't be so lucky."

Nurse Sarah dabbed a wound hard on Father Pat's forehead, and he said, "Ow, that hurts!"

Then she pushed his head back on the pillow, "Stop moving, and lie down, Father."

Mitch said, "Yeah, lie down, Father, or I'll knock you down again."

Father Pat shot back, "Just lay there while they stitch your manhood back on, boy-o."

"Right!" yelled Mitch, sitting up.

"Stop! Now. Both of you," said Dr Pete. Then he took the Betadine swab from the nurse who'd been dabbing Mitch's penis and held it in front of Mitch's face, slowly moving it closer and closer. Mitch retreated into the pillow.

Then, swishing the curtain back, Dr Pete approached Father Pat with the same implement: "Shut up, Pat, or I'll paint your face with his manhood."

Father Pat said, "I—uh—"

Dr Pete said, "Huh?" and pushed the swab forwards into Pat's face.

Father Pat retreated too.

"That's it, lay back down, Father Pat," said Dr Pete. "Open your mouth one more time, I'll stick this in. Got it?"

Father Pat nodded, meekly.

Dr Pete turned to Mitch, "Same goes for you. Got it?"

Mitch nodded, submissively.

The two patients lay back, contrite, both staring up at the small perforations in the white ceiling tiles.

Dr Pete returned to work on Mitch, flicking the corner of a smile to the nurses. They constrained their smirks as if it was part of their training, as much as wound cleaning and dressing – which they continued without further interruption from their unruly patients.

Dr Pete told Mitch that an infection had developed, but they were treating it. However, if Mitch moved again, he'd jeopardise the treatment, and make healing slower.

"Then there might be nothing we can do. And it could mean permanent damage," said Dr Pete, "So just relax. Don't move."

Then Dr Pete stepped over to Pat, prodded his friend's face and asked Nurse Sarah, "Fractures?"

Nurse Sarah said, "No."

"Lucky. Risk of concussion. Keep him here an hour," then to Pat, "Act your age. And your position."

With the nurses working away quietly, Dr Pete left Ward One. The sound of the radio gradually emerged from the silence, with a voice giving the end of a weather report. The nurses started chatting in Norf'k language as they worked.

"*Storm brewen*," said Nurse Lucy in Norf'k. ("Storm coming up, eh.")

"*Nawa noe cumen*," replied Nurse Lucy ("Yeah, came up unexpectedly.")

"*Si dar black cumen*," said Nurse Sarah. ("White squall. Started at sea.")

"*Nor-wes*," said Nurse Lucy. ("Nor-west.")

"*Cumen ukluns wae*," said Nurse Sarah. ("Headed our way, eh?")

"*Strorng win enna raen gwen pass east o uklun*," said Nurse Lucy. ("Big winds and rain but expected to pass east of us.")

"*En myse clorth orna line*," said Nurse Sarah. ("My washing's on the line.")

"*En mine*," said Nurse Lucy. ("Mine, too.")

They shrugged and smiled, "*Dars wuthen you get f' lewen at d' bass side orn earth*." ("That's what you get for living in paradise.")

When the nurses finished their work and were leaving Ward One, Nurse Lucy pulled back the dividing curtain and said to the two patients, "We're just outside, and we won't abide any disruptions. Or you're both straight out."

Twenty-seconds after they left, Father Pat suddenly frowned, and said, "Did you say your wife was on a boat?"

"Fuck off" came the response.

"Whoa!" said Father Pat.

"I told you she was with some fisherman who they reckon looks like Thor," said Mitch, "so if you're gonna niggle me, with my dick in bandage—on my fuckin' honeymoon—"

Father Pat said, "Charlie?"

Mitch said, "What?"

"Charlie Evans?"

"I dunno," said Mitch, "That maybe right."

Father Pat laughed and started to say, "For a start—"

Mitch interrupted, "Oh, fuck you. You've never been in love. You wouldn't understand."

"Whoa!" said Father Pat. "For a start, I've been in love plenty. I wasn't born a priest you know. I had some loves that'd make Shakespeare cry. And secondly—"

"And secondly, shut up," said Mitch.

"And secondly, Charlie Evans is more likely to fancy you, than your wife. Except he's happily married—"

"What the hell's that supposed to mean?"

Father Pat continued, "—to Dave Abbot."

Mitch was silent for moment, then said, "He's gay?"

"As springtime," said Father Pat.

"Oh, thank God," said Mitch.

"For his sake. And for his husband's sake," said Father Pat, "not just for your jealousy's sake."

Mitch said, "Oh yeah, that too."

"You really have a lot of work to do on this marriage stuff."

"That's rich, coming from you," said Mitch.

Father Pat said, "Don't worry, it's not all good news."

Mitch said, "What do you mean?"

"An unexpected storm at sea. It came out of nowhere. To the east of the island."

"Shit," said Mitch. He started to sit up, but yelled, "Ow!" before slumping back down. "It hurts."

Father Pat said, "Of course it does. You've had stitches and an infection."

Mitch tried to sit up again, "Ow."

"Where are you going?" said Father Pat.

"Down to the pier."

"To get wet?"

"Yeah."

"Why?"

"Because I gotta do something, old man," said Mitch, as he struggled to sit up without bending his middle. (Which when you think about sitting up, it's mainly about bending your middle.)

Eventually Mitch rolled like a sausage to the edge of the bed. Father Pat observed him with a bemused look.

Then, on his back, Mitch held the bedframe and swung his bare feet off the bed, which rolled him over onto his front. He squealed like a ghost.

"This is good entertainment," said Father Pat. "I could sell popcorn."

Mitch grunted and squealed and rolled over on to his back.

"How's getting wet going to help your wife?"

Mitch said, "Ow," and slid painfully over the edge of the bed. He arched backwards, grunting loudly, until his toes were touching the ground.

"You're going to get soaked in the storm and worsen your infection. Maybe cause permanent damage. How's that going to help Annie?" asked Father Pat.

Mitch was grunting too much to swear a response, as he tippy-toed his pale, white feet slowly forwards across one pale, lime lino tile.

"This is excruciating," said Father Pat. "Like watching performance art. Except worse."

Finally, Mitch was in a standing position with both hands behind him grasping the bed. His face was red, his gown was sticking to his body with sweat.

Father Pat said, "Well it only took you ten minutes to stand up. You should be down the pier by Christmas. Next year!" And he laughed aloud at his own joke.

Mitch said, "What do you suggest, smart-arse?"
Father Pat said, "Pray. Of course."
Mitch laughed.

CHAPTER THIRTY-THREE

SEA

Everyone's got a "worst storm" story.

No matter how bad a storm you've seen on land, it's nothing compared to a storm at sea. No matter how much your roof leaks and your windows shudder in a storm on land, your house probably isn't going to suddenly flip over and sink 1,000 metres to the bottom of the ocean.

In a storm at sea, it's all moving. Violently. Like it hates you. And when it overturns your vessel, you'll probably drown in about a minute, if you're lucky. One monstrous wave after another will pummel you like a team of underwater boxers, until you're exhausted. Maybe three horrific minutes, if you're very unlucky.

It's no mistake that the sea is described as "angry" during storms. The waves seem downright vindictive. The way it attacks us seems personal. As if the ocean has a mind of its own. And it's aiming all its bad moods at us.

The word for this storm at sea is "vengeful". Like it'd specifically targeted *Rainbow Warrior VI*, 60 kilometres off Norfolk Island, in order to flip it and absorb Charlie, Annie and the whole Arsehole family into the ocean's depths.

It hit them with crashing dumpers – slamming the *Rainbow Warrior VI* from starboard and port, jolting the passengers and crew from side to side – in the hope they'd fall overboard.

Chunky surface waves rattled it with speedbumps from beneath, to shake everyone loose, while the boat heeled and pitched erratically in the hope they'd fly out.

On a larger scale, the sea rose in monumental swells. They rose like the stadium surrounding a football field. Except liquid. And hateful. And coming for you.

Charlie had to churn the boat at a steep angle up these dangerous waves. Then, right at the peak of the stadium, there was a bulging lip of whitewash where the monster tried one last time to flick their boat over.

After that they were airborne – their stomachs near their ears – before dropping vertically down the other side of the wave at frightening speed.

The Arsehole family were below deck, repainting the cabin walls, and each other, with regurgitated sandwiches in the abstract expressionist style of Jackson Pollock.

Annie and Charlie were above deck, in the wheelhouse, holding tight to stay upright. Both had zippered their bright yellow foul-weather jackets. Both were staring fixedly at the mean seas around them.

Annie said, "How'd it come up so fast?"

"She doesn't know the rules, Annie," said Charlie, "doesn't watch the weather report. She *is* the weather. Makes it up as she goes. Always changing. Better call it in. Getting hairy."

Charlie pressed the call button on the handset to his right and spoke loudly at it, "Norfolk Base, this is *Rainbow Warrior Six*. Come in Norfolk Base. Over."

The static crackled. Then a weak voice from the radio said, "*Rainbow Warrior Six*, this is Norfolk Base. Hey there, Charlie. Over."

"Hey base, we got weather out here. Wind from North Nor-east, thirty-six to forty knots. Over."

"On the radar now, *Rainbow Six*. Came out of nowhere, eh? Over."

"You're telling me! We're one hundred-and-eighty-four-degrees latitude; ninety-three-point-seven degrees longitude. Four passengers in distress below decks—names on manifest with office. And geez, it's peeling! Hang on."

Charlie focused on steering a straight course down the current monster. He had to fight the wheel so the boat didn't get pushed on an angle and roll.

When the boat was safely under its own power again, in the trough between monsters, Charlie spoke at the radio once more, "Sorry, Base. There's also me as skipper, and new deckie, Annie—umh," Charlie glanced at Annie.

Annie said, "Adams."

Charlie nodded, "Annie Adams."

"Got it, *Rainbow Six*. There's—"

Suddenly static filled the airwaves.

Charlie pressed the call again, and said, "Norfolk Base, this is *Rainbow Warrior Six*, come in Norfolk Base. Over."

There was nothing except crackles. Charlie tweaked some knobs and caught some syllables but no coherent sentences.

"Norfolk Base, this is *Rainbow Warrior*—" then steering sharply, said, "geez this is coming up. Better get the—"

The radio interrupted, "*Rainbow Warrior Six*, this is Norfolk Base, do you read? Over."

"Norfolk Base, this is *Rainbow Warrior Six*, not read-ing you clearly. Comms cutting out. We're heading south sou-west towards home at speed. Under very heavy weather. Close to fifty knot winds. Over."

"*Rainbow Warrior Six*, Norfolk Base here, we're not reading you clearly, but we'll keep this channel—"

There was loud white noise. Then nothing more.

Charlie tried the tweak with the dials again, but the swaying of the boat caused his hand to swing past the ra-dio too fast to catch the knobs. He needed both hands to drive the boat up and down the malevolent waves, so he gave up on the radio to steer with his left hand and throttle with his right.

The radio crackled loudly. The storm shrieked louder.

Annie felt useless and afraid. All her energy was spent just standing upright and holding the centre pole where the wheelhouse opened to the rear deck.

Charlie turned and yelled, "Get the safety line from the box."

Annie yelled, "What?"

Charlie flicked his finger at a marine storage box stick-ing up out of the deck. Then he returned his hand to the wheel as quickly as possible.

The aft deck, behind the half-cabin wheelhouse, was two metres long by two metres wide – about the size of a king-sized mattress. (A leaky waterbed mattress. On a hate-ful ocean of treacherous water. Under a ceiling of pelting rain.)

The white epoxy fibreglass storage box was halfway along the deck on the port side. Annie stared back it from where she was standing, holding the pole, which was hold-ing up the roof of the wheelhouse.

It was only a metre away, to the right, from Annie. But it looked much further.

Annie started moving, but as soon as her right shoe lifted off the deck, the sea took the chance to knock her off her feet. It hurled her down hard, slamming the deck.

Winded, Annie was pushed around the deck on her back, bouncing off each edge of the confined space like a snooker ball butting all four cushions. Except these weren't cushions. These were thick fibreglass surfaces, hardened with marine epoxy. And Annie was bouncing off their sharp edges with her arms, legs and ribs.

Annie completed her first lap around the deck and was about to be sent spinning for another round, but managed to grab the storage box with both arms as she slid past. She hung to it, like a drowning woman clinging to a floating buoy. Her legs mopped the sopping deck – swinging left and right like windscreen-wipers.

"Stop messing about," yelled Charlie, smiling down at her from the wheelhouse.

Annie couldn't afford the energy to smile back. Her arms were holding on with all her might. She was terrified the forces of sea and storm would be too strong for her and rip her away from the boat.

She was afraid for her life, in a new way. She'd been shaken in a plane and pinned by a cow, but those situations were beyond her control. Here, her survival was totally dependent on how hard she could cling to this stupid, hard, slippery box. In an instant, things got life-and-death serious. In the flick of a wave she could be gone.

And there was that ancient, weakening thought – right in her face – that the task was beyond her. Some crazy part of her was actually yelling, *Let go. Just let go.*

Suddenly, she realised there were no rules to life: *Not how good, or how deserving I am,* she thought, *All that matters is how hard I can hold a box. And I want to live.*

And she thought of Mitch. That if she died now, she'd never see him again. And that thought almost made her suicidal, but suicidal to live. Ego death. She'd do anything to live. You only see it when you're that close to the edge. She no longer cared if she lived or died, she'd put it all on the line to try.

And in that instant, washing the aft deck of a fishing boat in a storm at sea, one muscle reflex away from death, Annie wished she'd made love with Mitch on the pool deck, and bugger the Arsehole family. She was furious to live.

Ain't love grand?

She wasn't afraid of dying as much as not seeing her beloved.

The human heart – what a creature! So wild, so much passion in such a tiny organ. So much love, it can make us rise up against an impossible storm at sea. Shout "Fuck you" to an inevitable death. And make the miracle start. Love, the miracle maker.

In that thought of love, Annie's heart clenched. And her survival began.

Her stomach muscles clenched.

Her torso and shoulders clenched.

Her face clenched. And her knees bent and her legs swung one last mopping arc, then she humped with the momentum and rode a jolt of the boat, to wrap herself around that box. She absorbed the storage box and stuck to it.

If there was a class on how to stick to a storage box aboard a boat knocking and flicking in a furious ocean storm, this would be the method. There'd be an illustration of Annie wrapped around that box.

In this perfect manoeuvre, her body adopted the shape of the box. She swung with it – left and right, and up and down – like she was its lid.

Unfortunately, she wasn't its lid. She had to get off the box, somehow, in order to *open* the lid. And she had to do it soon.

She was adopting the most energy efficient pose for holding onto a bucking box on a boat in a storm, but her muscles wouldn't last much longer. Lactic acid was burning her arms and back, and her legs and hips and neck. Her power was draining like the rain that was falling off her.

CHAPTER THIRTY-FOUR

WARD

Leaning on his bed, Mitch said, "Pray! What good's that gonna do?"

Father Pat, still lying in bed with a patch over his eye, was about to respond when Nurse Sarah came into Ward One, and went to Mitch's side and asked quietly, "Is your wife on Charlie Evans's boat?"

"Yes," said Mitch, "I think so."

Nurse Sarah said, "We got a call from the Norfolk Base of the national Rescue Coordination Centre. Charlie called them about ten minutes ago. A squall has kicked up unexpectedly, and they're caught in it. But they're safe and they're heading back to Norfolk."

"But," said Mitch, "but—umh—they—"

"That's all they said."

"Shit. Are they in danger?"

"Charlie called in as a precaution."

Mitch paused, then asked, "What's a squall?"

"A sudden storm," replied Nurse Sarah.

"Is there an emergency helicopter?"

"No, it has to fly out from Australia."

"No emergency helicopter? But we're surrounded by ocean!" Mitch was looking really worried now.

"I know."

"We can take it up with the Australian government, later," said Father Pat, "But for now, search and rescue is organised out of Australia. Probably Canberra."

"How long will that take?"

Nurse Sarah answered, "Three, or four hours."

"Shit. Can I speak to her?"

Nurse Sarah looked at Father Pat for a way to soften the blow, but there wasn't one: "No, the comms are down."

"Comms are down?"

"That happens in storms," said Father Pat.

"What about sending a boat out to find them?"

"They can't send a boat out in a storm," said Nurse Sarah.

"What the fuck can we do then?"

Nurse Sarah looked at Father Pat, who looked at Mitch and said, "You asked, 'why pray?' The answer is, because sometimes it's all you can do."

"Shit—fuck—shit—" said Mitch angrily. Then he lowered his head and clenched his face to keep the tears in. The sound of a wild animal in agony rose from his clenched jaw. Then he exhaled and looked up at Pat and said, "What do we say?"

CHAPTER THIRTY-FIVE

BOAT

Annie clenched the storage box and heard Charlie's voice above the roar of the storm, "You right?"

She grunted and glanced at Charlie. Saw a world of angry water. Grand Canyons of wet war. Saw walls of swell standing straight up, charging with hatred against other equally angry walls of water.

Annie felt a balance tip, a gyroscope spinning off-centre inside her.

She squinted. Saw Charlie's concerned eyes shining from the shadow of his flapping hood surrounded by mist and, behind his left shoulder, an impossibly huge wave breaking at the top of a water mountain.

Annie gulped at it for a heartbeat – trying to comprehend its size, proximity, and trajectory – then felt her stomach hollow out in awe. Then, every fibre of every muscle instinctively clenched the box for life.

Charlie saw the look on her face and spun to face the monster, "Oh yeah," he said. "She's a big 'un. Hold on."

Vertical, the boat leaned back, and sped upwards. The axis of everything shifted; Annie's internal gyroscope was sent spinning at such a fine angle she could hear the shriek-ing sound it made. But it was actually her voice.

She clenched her eyes and tucked her head against the epoxy fibreglass box. Pulled herself deeper into the hard, wet, slippery surface, to merge the atoms of her skin with the molecules of resin fibreglass. She was suddenly verti-cal, and her fingernails dug into the shiny surface for 25 micrometre's purchase in the hard gelcoat surface.

Annie's pulse hammered a speedcore beat in her ears. Her internal gyroscope was shrieking horror-opera vocals. The ocean crashed a death-metal calamity with revenge lyrics. And above it all, she could hear Charlie screaming, "Yahoooooooooo!"

CHAPTER THIRTY-SIX

WARD

Horizontal in the hospital bed, Mitch pushed his head back into the deep pillows. Absorbed in the cool and comfortable dimple of white cotton, it should've been relaxing. But he was pushing hard, and straining, and it still wouldn't stop the emergency of fears about his wife. His fantasies to save her, spooled on an endless reel:

- pluck her from the boat by a helicopter;

- swing over from another boat on a bendy pole;

- drop down a hook from the clouds;

- or just stand on the pier, getting drenched, staring hate at the wild seas.

Truth is, he couldn't do any of it. He couldn't even get out of bed. He pushed his hand against his groin, into immediate pain shooting along fifteen different nerves, sparking out in a star of agony that was over the edge of intolerable but somehow slightly better than the pain in his heart.

He was in a storm inside. She was in a real storm, outside. His guts flip-flopped. His chest viced inwards in shrieking pain. A headache screamed in the eye of the cyclone of damned possibilities.

Then he felt the ring on the tip of his forefinger. Felt it being twisting by his thumb.

He lifted his hand and looked at it. Slipped the gold ring of white teeth off his finger. Looked into deeply. Kissed it. Held it to his lips, hard.

It stopped the cyclone. Or at least inflated a secure bubble of love from his heart. Just for a moment. He melted in affection.

He felt it with his fingertips and focused his third eye on this ugly, outrageous artefact that was so much more than jewellery.

It was a signifier of the depths he'd dive for her. The risks he'd take. The sacrifices he'd make. And the stupidity of those risks.

He'd thrust his hand into dark coral and been bitten. And it could've been much worse. What would it'd mattered if he'd let the ring fall? Come back later? Forgotten it completely?

Instead, he'd risked his life and, ironically, the relationship itself. For what? To be her hero? To prove his love?

So the ring meant both things: The romance and the reality.

And here he was considering impulses, again. To what? Stand in the rain? Make a meaningless gesture? A symbol for her. When what's required wasn't passion, but intelligence. Commitment. Restraint. The big picture.

Loving Annie didn't mean *showing* how much he'd do for her. It meant *doing* what was best for her. And him. Being safe for her.

Not heroics. Not gestures.

The real proof of his love was doing the smart thing. The best thing for them both. Which in this case was recuperating. Like the stupid priest said.

I can do anything for her, he thought, *but can I do nothing?*

Love squeezed Mitch's heart, choked his throat, and formed tears in his eyes.

"I don't know what to say," he said. "What do we say?"

"Eh?"

"Of course, I'll pray," said Mitch. "I'll do anything. Everything."

Father Pat said, "What's your heart say?"

"God, please look after her. God, please look after her. God, please look after her," said Mitch. Then he closed his eyes and went there. It was easy. His heart saying words in his ears, "Please, God, please look after her. God, please look after her. God, please look after her. God, please—"

He opened his eyes on the gold ring encircled by the white jaw of little teeth. And he felt it. Knew deeply, something he believed in. His wife. Their love. And the phenomenal mysteries of this life – beyond anything in any sci-fi movie, or song.

Mitch looked at the ring and said, "You couldn't write this shit." Then he held it to his lips and prayed to the deep mysteries, far beyond his misunderstandings. And he called upon that love from the deepest ocean in the world. He whispered into the ring, like it was a portal to that God, out there in the space between life and death, in the infinity beyond. Mitch spoke into the ring of teeth like it was a phone, "God, God, God, please, please, please—God, please, please, please help her."

CHAPTER THIRTY-SEVEN

BOAT

She heard it inside her.

"I NEED THAT CABLE, ANNIE!"

Time travelled so fast, every minute was an hour of thought and emotion; of life-and-death reflexes; of mind-boggling revelations about gravity, nature, and the physics of chaos.

She told herself it was just a thought. An imagined voice in her head. Surely Charlie couldn't *actually* be asking her to move.

Surely!

The water car-washed her from all directions. Her muscles contracted with every wave, and swerve and tilt, like she was riding a hard bucking bull. In an earthquake. Over depthless liquid death.

A square, shiny, slippery bull with no handles and sharp edges. It pulsed to buck her. Pulsed her painfully. Wanted her dead.

She held herself tight to the box, but it jolted any tiny gap in her grip, and smashed her bones back down.

She had to thrust hard against the rigid surface to reconnect. Each bucking thrust smashed her bones, her shin, her chin, her pelvis, her chest bone, her ear. She slammed down with each almighty jolt. Slammed with force like someone had hold of her ribs, or head, and was pulling it back from the box, then slamming it down with the full force of their strength. Time and again. Smashing her against the hard fibreglass, time and again.

And it was like there was another set of hands wriggling her from side to side to dislodge her. It wanted to send her flying off the boat. The ocean wanted her.

Her muscles felt like they were bleeding.

She heard, "Safety line," above the shrieking storm.

She heard it again but chose to believe it was imagined. *Surely Charlie couldn't. Surely.*

She chanced a glance. Timed it as the boat slumped into the valley between two monsters, when the centrifugal force pushed her into the box. If she moved her head now, it mightn't lift much, but also wouldn't be smashed back into the box too much.

She strained her neck against the force. And squinted upwards.

CHAPTER THIRTY-EIGHT

WARD

Lying in Bed Two of Ward One, Mitch didn't know which direction was north.

He had no idea where the hospital was on the island, let alone which direction it faced. But he looked at the windows and hoped – by mystery beyond sci-fi – that he was gazing east, in the direction where Annie was in a storm at sea.

Not that he could even see the sea. All he could see was rain splashing the windows, like they were in a car wash. Beyond that, the palm trees frantically waved in the wind, as if signalling their distress.

He imagined he could hear them screaming for help.

Not that he could help. Not the stupid bloody palm trees and, more importantly, not his beautiful new wife.

"I'm going now, lad," said Father Pat.

"In this?"

"I'm not made of paper," said Father Pat.

"What good's getting wet gonna do?" said Mitch. "To quote some wise old priest."

"Hah! You'll keep, son," said Father Pat, "I've got to go and reassure people."

"How?"

"Radio station," said Father Pat.

"Oh," said Mitch. Then after a beat, he said, "Wait! Why did the comms go down on the boat?"

"Not sure," said Father Pat. "There's always bad satellite interference during big storms. And maybe the radio on the boat was—" He stopped as soon as he said it, so as not to incite fear. But too late. Mitch had instantly imagined a kaleidoscope of tragedies that could have damaged the boat's radio.

"Jesus, I gotta find out," said Mitch, and he started up again.

"Oh no," said Father Pat, "not this again."

"I gotta reassure her," said Mitch. "It's something I can do."

"Whoa, whoa," said Father Pat with palms outstretched forward in a calming gesture. Then he said, softly, "The comm's ain't working, Mitch. They're not working. Satellite cuts out during storms."

Mitch's mind was racing, "OK—OK—" he said. Then blurted out, "Has someone got a ham radio?"

The priest stopped. Paused. Looked upwards and squinted, and said, "The radio station would be able to transmit the signal."

"Yes," said Mitch. "Even better."

"I'll call Darls," said the priest. He pulled out his mobile, and saw the network was out, and said, "Fuck," then walked to the door and met Nurse Sarah, "Sarah, have we got a landline?"

"Sure," said Sarah, "in reception."

Father Pat looked at Mitch and said, "Can you make it?"

"Ha! Of course I can make it, you old fart," said Mitch. "Can *you* make it?"

Pat laughed. And Mitch laughed. Then gasped in pain.

Pat went to him, caught him under the shoulder, and they looked at each other and laughed through fatigue and stress.

Sarah looked at two of the weirdest patients she'd had in years – her childhood priest and a young, bandaged, new-lywed tourist in a bulging gown. Two men who'd hated each other an hour ago, now holding each other's shoulder, alternately laughing, and wincing in pain.

"Sarah," said Father Pat, "we're going to call the radio station and try to send a message to the *Rainbow*."

"I'll get the wheelchair," she said.

CHAPTER THIRTY-NINE
RECEPTION

Father Pat's Hush Puppies squelched quickly along the lino tiles of the corridor and into the waiting room where Roz sat behind the reception counter.

"Roz, my love," said Father Pat, "may we use the phone to call the radio?"

"Sure," said Roz, "Making a request, Father Pat?"

"No, my dear, it's a bit more serious than that. This storm's blowing up terribly, and the comms are out as you know. We need to reassure some people."

"Yes, of course, Father."

"And there's some people caught out there in the teeth of it. My fella, Mitch, wants to get word to his wife, out there."

"OK," she said. Then suddenly yelled, "Wait! What? Who? Not that crazy bitch who hit me?"

"Now, Roz."

"She's crazy. She bit his dick off—excuse me, Father, but everyone's saying it was my fault 'cos I slept with him. Which I never did!"

"Of course, love. We all know you didn't do anything wrong."

"No, I've got a lot of calls, Father Pat. Gotta keep this line open for emergencies."

CHAPTER FORTY

BOAT

The boat was heaving. Annie's muscles were giving out. She could barely see Charlie standing two metres away under the canopy of the wheelhouse. There was a thick wall of water between them, and darts of rain were spiking her face and eyes.

But she could no longer deny that Charlie was shouting above the din, "Safety line! Safety line!"

Fuck, she thought, and hot terror suddenly burned her throat and neck. She felt fear burning deeper into her chest, like acid corroding her soft organs; her heart, her lungs.

In a world of storm around her, all Annie could see was the fear inside.

Then she heard the skipper again, and glancing there, glimpsed his washed-out shape through slanted pellets.

He was facing forwards, one hand on the wheel, one fist pumping air in front of him, like a soccer player who'd scored a goal.

Then she discerned his voice above the squall: "Yahoo! Come on, baby. *Yahoooo*!"

The shock stopped her. All her attention went to Charlie through a tunnel of focus.

"What are you doing?" she screamed.

Charlie turned quickly, "Yahooooo! This is what I live for, Annie." Then turning to face the wheel, he screamed, "Yahoooo-eeeee-aaaaaagh!"

She gasped laughter. A chilled exhalation of amazement shocked her lungs wide open. "He's not afraid," she thought, "He's excited."

The fear suddenly flipped inside her.

Her muscles reacted immediately. She raised her head in a powerful yoga pose, that lifted her chest with a push-up that locked her strong arms into a triangle that counteracted jolts from all sides. Then her knees sprung out, her thighs spread, and she straddled the box.

Then, concentrating on the movement of the boat, she was instantly aware of the larger rhythms of the storm chaos.

Her gyroscope was back and spinning in equilibrium within her solar plexus. Her senses were suddenly attuned: eyes, ears, fingers, muscles.

Feeling the wind direction on the wet skin of her face.

Feeling the powerful forces surge inside her.

Hearing a rhythmic beat, underneath all that distorted, death-metal jazz.

Feeling the swell peak, under the boat, then feeling it yield to a momentary drop in intensity.

And in that breath, she flowed: shot her left hand towards a chrome rail. In a microsecond's pulse, she grasped it, swung her legs off the box, curled her knees into her chest, and used the rhythm of her environment to slide off and drop down into a small space between the box and the wall of the aft deck.

Her knees crunched onto the deck, hard, but it was a pain of safety and Annie wedged in tight. From this position she was able to access the box.

"Yahoo!" she howled.

She heard Charlie's "Yahoo!" in response.

Annie felt the rhythm of the ride. Crowd-surfing a mosh pit of terrible gods. The tyrannous punk children of Neptune and Salacia. Or Poseidon and Amphitrite. Or Tūwhiri and Paraweranui.

CHAPTER FORTY-ONE

RECEPTION

"Roz," said Father Pat.

But Roz ignored him, and spoke into her headset, "Oh hello, Margaret. *Wataweih?*"

"Roz," repeated the priest.

"Got some blow to it, hasn't it, Margaret—" said Roz.

Then Margaret's voice suddenly filled the reception on speakerphone, "Oh yes, dear. It's a big 'un."

Roz's head wobbled, as she looked around the room for the source of the sound. Then she looked down at her phone console and stopped. There was Father Pat's finger pressing the speakerphone button.

Father Pat yelled, "Sorry Margaret, it's Pat here. We'll call ya' back, darlin'. We've got an emergency. Roz has to save the day."

"OK, dearie, bye," said Margaret's voice.

"Bye," said Pat.

Roz's face lit red. She was about to explode indignant workplace authority, but Pat looked her straight in the eyes and said firmly, "Don't."

Roz paused and her eyes widened.

Father Pat said, "I remember when your mum broke her leg, and you called the ambo. Remember that? You must've been only five. Or was it six?"

"Six," said Roz.

"Six years old and such courage," said Father Pat. "I know your feelings got hurt, yesterday, Rozzy. But this man hurts for real. It was an eel that bit him. And his wife—they've only been married two days. Two days married! Now, she's in peril. Hear me? Grave. Danger. He might never see her again. Might never hear her again. You want to get in the way of that, Rozzy?"

Roz shook her head.

"Well, it's time for your courage again, my love," said Father Pat. "You're the only one who can help them. Only you, Rozzy. Only you. We need you to be the hero, again, my love. We need you to call Darls at the radio station and tell her we need an emergency announcement."

CHAPTER FORTY-TWO

BOAT

The boat was pumping up and down, like the Weather God's wind children were dancing in the mosh pit under it. As if the punk god kids were celebrating Annie's excitement with renewed fervour. Now they're concerting to bounce her, and the boat, up and down; like the game where you fling someone up and down from a blanket.

One of them, Apū-hau, is singing, "Pump it up! Pump it up!"

Except the blanket is 10 million square kilometres in area. And the upsurging force is a trillion tonnes per square centimetre of death-defying fun across a 40 square metre boat.

Apū-hau's brother, Ao-tākawe, joins the chorus, "Pump up the volume! Pump up the volume!"

But Annie is squeezed in the crevice between the box and the gunwale and can withstand the action. She inflates her muscles and expands her chest to wedge herself tighter into the space.

Tiny breaths, drawn sharply between clenched teeth. Then, in slow motion, she moves her hand forwards, in a wildly swaying gesture towards the latch of the box. She snarls a breath and inflates to fill the space. Focusing all her energy on her swaying arm, she reaches the box and uses the motion of the waves to help her lift the lid.

The lid opens up and bites down again, hard, like the chomping jaw of a snapping turtle. A heavy fibreglass one, with a wide gaping gob.

Annie's hand gets caught in the chomping jaws. She wrenches it loose and the lid slams down, again, smashing her thumb nail.

"Faaaarck," yells Annie.

Then she sucks her thumb and waves with her other hand to Charlie, whom she knew would've looked over out of concern.

She's already too focused on improving her next attempt at opening the lid to look his way. And after the worst of the sharp pain recedes, Annie inhales a short gasp, and centres around moving her hand to the lid, lifting it, and holding it from flying away.

CHAPTER FORTY-THREE

RECEPTION

Nurse Sarah wheeled Mitch into reception. Father Pat was standing in front of the counter talking into Roz's speakerphone.

"Yes, Darls, we've been doing this forever on Norfolk," said Father Pat towards the phone. "This is a seafaring community. We live and die by it. Now there's a boat out there, in a cyclone. No comms. Four tourists and a young, newly married girl, and our beloved Charlie Evans. We need to make contact. Now! This is what we do on Norfolk Island."

"I know all that, Pat," said Darls's voice through the phone, "I do. And I sympathise. But this is way beyond the radio station's charter."

"This is Norfolk, Darls. Not Canberra," said Father Pat. "We're the ones stuck out here in the world's biggest ocean. Not the politicians"

"I know where we are, Pat," said Darls's voice, "but this is my job."

Then Roz talked towards the speakerphone, "They used to sing to them, you know, Darls?"

"What?" said Darls.

"The women," said Roz. "You know this, Darls. Our grandmothers. My great-nan. Standing on the cliffs, singing their men home when they couldn't see the island."

"Yes, I know the story, Roz," said Darls.

"Nothing's changed, except the technology," said Roz. "We're just singing them home."

There was silence, then Darls said, "Fuck. Alright, alright!"

"Good on you, Darls," said Roz.

"But how?" said Darls's voice.

"Short wave through the antenna!" said Mitch.

"Who's that?" asked Darls.

Father Pat said, "Mitch, the young fella whose wife's on the boat."

Silence.

"OK," said Darls, "it's worth a shot. But who knows ham radio—oh, shit, don't answer that. Shorty does."

"Yep, Shorty," said Father Pat.

"Shit," said Darls, "OK, but you better defend me when they try to sack me for this, Pat. You, too, Roz. And you, too, whatever your name is."

"We will," said Roz.

"Me too," said Nurse Sarah.

"Cripes," said Darls. "You got the whole town there?"

"It's a community service announcement," said Father Pat.

"About public safety," added Mitch.

"And an emergency announcement," chimed in Nurse Sarah.

"Yes, that's good. An emergency announcement. Community service. Good stuff. OK. Can you get onto Shorty, please, Roz," said Darls.

"Sure can, Annie. I'll put you on hold."

CHAPTER FORTY-FOUR

RADIO

Inside the little radio station under the huge antenna, in the middle of the green paddock spotted with cows, Patsy Cline was singing "Crazy".

Darls was sitting at the announcer's desk, moving her fingertips in tiny circles at her temples, whispering to no one, "You got that right, Patsy."

She shook her head, breathed deeply, and reached for her necklace of Ta'aroa. She rubbed the small cowrie shell, looked up to the ceiling and offered her little prayer to the broadcast gods for her message to be clear and helpful.

Then she looked at the desk, switched the fader from Patsy to herself, and said into the microphone, "Sorry for the interruption, Patsy, but we have an emergency announcement. A dangerous weather warning. And a public safety announcement."

ལྗཽ

In the waiting room of Norfolk Island Hospital, Roz, Mitch, Nurse Sarah and Father Pat were all looking at the radio speaker.

"She's covering all the bases," said Roz.

"Good girl," said Father Pat.

ભ₰

In the studio of Norfolk Island Radio, Darls spoke into the microphone: "As yorle know, a big storm has whipped-up and is coming this way from the nor-nor-east. We want yorle to batten down the hatches because, by all indications, she's packing over 80 kilometre an hour winds, with a big surf and sideways rain. Stay off the roads if you can. Tidy up any loose things around the yard. Make sure yorle have a torch with batteries and yorle phones are charged. And of course, now's definitely not the time to go onto the water for any reason. In fact, that's the second part of this community emergency announcement."

ભ₰

Father Pat smiled at Roz and said, "Good on you, Roz."

Roz blushed, then shyly glanced over at Mitch, and said, "You better come around here, Mitch. Closer to the phone. I'll move Arlene's chair so the wheelchair can slot-in under the desk."

Nurse Sarah wheeled Mitch behind the desk. "Thanks," he said, then looked intently at the phone, which was on hold to the island's one and only radio station, where Darls was on-air explaining to the populace in every car, house, café, and office, the revolutionary action they were attempting.

Darls said, "Comms are down and we've lost contact with Charlie Evans's boat. So we're going to use the broad-

cast antenna, here, on top of Norfolk Radio, to try to connect with *Rainbow Warrior Six*."

CHAPTER FORTY-FIVE
STATION

Darls sat in the little studio under the big antenna and spoke carefully into the mic: "We Norfolk sullen, we help each other with whatever we can muddle together. In this case, it's the good old radio. So, while we're waiting for Shorty to help us with this short-wave experiment, I think it's good to remember, here on Norfolk Island, the sea is our home."

In Bung's house, high on the cliff, overlooking the stormy sea, the old soldier looked at his radio, and heard Darls saying, "She's our mother. We live and die by her grace. We inherit her beauty and bounty. And also, at times like this, her wrath. And when one of us is lost out there, we need to help them get home."

In Prinke, the organic café and eco store, Sharyn, the Earth Mother, and all her gourmet goddesses stopped what they were doing and stared at the Bluetooth speaker behind the counter. Sharyn put down the bag of activated almonds she was hauling and looked at the radio. Monet stopped barista-ing. Danielle stopped shaping caramel mocha energy balls. And all the customers stopped talking and looked towards the speaker.

In Max's Department Store, the shoppers stopped shopping and looked at the transistor radio hanging from a beam next to the register.

In Pete's Place, Pete stopped counting the money at the cash register.

In Carmel's Wool Supplies, Carmel stopped knitting.

In KK's Gym, Kel was describing to his personal-training client the proper way to execute a bicep-curl. But he stopped mid curl and instead focused his attention on the radio playing in the background.

In Candy's Yoga Studio, Candy stopped yoga-ing. She stood and walked towards the radio next to the Buddha statue. The eyes of all her yoga students followed her, watching as she turned up the volume. Then they all copied her movements and sat quietly in Sukhasana and listened.

In Norfolk Mechanical, Dave slid out from under a Landcruiser, sat up, and looked at the portable radio hanging from a hook on the garage wall.

In Slick and Sons Butcher, Pete, Kyle, and the boys stopped serving and joking and cutting and cleaning, and all swung their attention to the radio in the back room where Wes had turned it up.

In Wunna Ts, Rick stopped screen-printing a T-shirt and looked up at his wife Cath at the counter, who raised her eyebrows and turned up the volume.

In the office of Christian-Bailey's Hardware, George and Smiley both looked up from their desks at the same moment and turned to the radio.

In Government House, George, the Administrator, excused himself from his guests and walked into the kitchen and listened to the radio with the chef, James, and the waitresses, Tay and Eve.

Drew the barber stopped barbering.

Naomi at The Olive Cafe, stopped cooking and leant across the counter to turn up the radio.

Alex, the owner-builder, on the roof of Glencar Villas, waved at Hunky, the carpenter, who stopped hammering; they both looked at the paint-splattered radio perched on the scaffolding.

Mary, sitting on the couch of her sunroom with little Tom-tom, stopped reading *Mitty the Duck* and said, "Go turn the radio up for me please, little one." Tom-tom jumped up and scampered into the kitchen, climbed onto the bench and reached up to the radio and tweaked the volume.

And they all heard Darls saying, "I was reminded by Roz, the receptionist, up at the hospital just now, that this is what we've always done on Norfolk Island.

"Back in the whaling days of my grandfather, my Da and maybe yours, too, worked on small boats hunting huge animals on the largest ocean in all conditions. Sometimes two or three days and nights at a time. Six men in a small wooden row-boat hunting whales – the world's biggest animal. They'd be turned around by the chase. Blown about by storms. They'd be towed over the horizon, and over another horizon, and over another one.

"In mountainous seas, when the sky was wet and grey, they couldn't see the stars to guide them back to Norfolk Island. And if they were lucky—and the whale was not—they'd turn and head for home, with no way of knowing which direction that was. All they had was instinct, twelve tired arms and a fifty-tonne deadweight to tow. Damaged equipment and damaged men, under a sky full of clouds in a sea full of sharks.

"Back then, our mums and nans and great-grandmothers would light lanterns on the cliffs of Norfolk Island. Then they'd all stand there and sing. They'd all stand there, along the cliffs, in the rain, and sing this song into the dark of night and out to the stormy seas. A song of hope that, somewhere out there in the dark, their crews could hear the tune and follow their voices back home.

"You know this one, they'd also sing it over our cribs when we were bubs trying to sleep. I'll play it now while we twiddle some knobs and try to link up with our man, Charlie, and his crew aboard the *Rainbow Warrior Six*, somewhere out there in this squall."

Darls faded out. Then, on all those radios, in all those stores and houses and cars all over Norfolk Island, the hymn "Brightly Beams Our Father's Mercy" swelled from everyone's speakers.

And a few quiet tears ran down those listeners' cheeks.

CHAPTER FORTY-SIX

BOAT

The *Rainbow Warrior VI* was bobbing like a cork in a washing machine. Jostled and tossed, but somehow still floating and somehow still upright.

Annie shook her head in wonder as she felt her stomach rise with the little boat over another monster. She lifted the lid of the box again, and extended her arm straight out like a beam so the lid was fully open. All her body was muscled towards keeping the lid ajar, as they fell through a hole in gravity, and fell over the cliff of yet another wave-mountain.

When they bottomed out in the trough, Annie's body and the lid were pushed down by the force of inertia, but her arm remained locked. *Like steel*, she thought, *like steel*.

In the next breath, she forced her other arm up and over the lid of the storage box, and finger-delved for whatever the hell a "safety line" felt like.

Her fingers became entangled with shapes that boggled her imagination as her body was shaken. Then, when gravity allowed, she strained her neck muscles to lift her head so she could peek into the box.

Charlie glanced over and shouted, "Two safety lines. Now! They're black!"

CHAPTER FORTY-SEVEN
BELOW

Below deck, the Arsehole family were a mess. All four were strewn on the floor, along with everything else in the small cabin.

The only things that hadn't fallen were four dinner plates, miraculously still standing on a shelf in the tiny galley, rattling against their flimsy timber stay.

All the other plates, cups and glasses had already smashed, adding dangerous hazards to the stew of people, fruit, cutlery, clothing, snorkelling equipment, vomit, electronic equipment, toilet paper, books, and sandwiches.

It was an acutely dangerous situation for the Arseholes. They were at the filthy, jagged, pointy end of a dire emergency. Their lives were flipping end over end in a coin toss for life and death.

Until now, it was just Mr and Mrs Arsehole who knew how close to death they were. Now, as the motion of the ocean flung their wrecked bodies around and round, and up and down, and into each other, and through the spew, and gasping through rubbish to breathe, Brooklyn and Hugh Junior became aware of their predicament, too.

Out of respect for these so-nearly departed souls, it's time to use their proper names. They are the Brown family from England.

Mr Hugh Brown is a plastic surgeon who wears a bow tie to the Nottingham private hospital where he works. His wife, Marjory, is an interior designer and respectable amateur tennis player. Brooklyn Louise Brown, aged 14, is in year 10, where she excels in mathematics and hockey, and is in love with Tony Buchanan, the sports captain, whose actual girlfriend, Rachel Bourke, is Brooklyn's best friend. Hugh Brown Junior, aged 11, has spent most of his first year of senior school being bullied on the school bus, but he fantasises about exacting his bloody revenge while playing *Call of Duty*.

The Browns live in a small regional town, called Pury End, in East Midlands, UK. None of them has confessed their love for that quaint little hamlet in their day-to-day lives. But right now, each of them would give anything – all their assets, their house, Hugh's club memberships, Marjory's trophies, Brooklyn's sports captain, Hugh Junior's PlayStation III, all their hair and probably most of their toes – to be back in their boring little hamlet near Towcester.

CHAPTER FORTY-EIGHT

RECEPTION

Staff and visitors from all around the hospital were gathering in the reception and waiting room. They all looked up at the speakers, which played a 2007 recording of the hymn "Brightly Beams" sung by the a cappella group, Choral Reef, singing in a four-part harmony:

> Let the lower lights be burning;
> Send a gleam across the wave.
> Some poor fainting, struggling seaman
> You may rescue, you may save.

CHAPTER FORTY-NINE
SHORTY

There's a country road on Norfolk Island where all the house names include the word "Roof". It was a joke that spread down the street. A cultural phenomenon that's gained anthropological acclaim in universities in Australia and New Zealand. An unorganised, organic relay of humour in a tight, neighbourly community.

There's "Red Roof", "Rusty Roof", and "Under the Roof". The sign outside the church house is "Holey Roof". And down the end of this street, there's a place called, "Low Roof", which belongs to Shorty, who got his name because he's the tallest man on the island.

It's a smart house nestled in a grove of white oaks and fruit trees. It has a view of the valley with a forest of trees spanning the entire palette of greens.

Inside, the design style is function over form. There's minimal furniture and maximal contraptions. In the space between the two lounge chairs is an oscilloscope. On the old cathode-ray TV is a Crooke's Tube. On the kitchen table is a radiometer.

The cupboards are stocked with Pyrex beakers and cylinders, but there's only two plates for food, and two cups for drinking. Shorty bought two of each because he wanted to encourage visitors but found more than one at a time overwhelming.

His network of contraptions and mysterious boxes with dials and meters are connected by wires threading from room to room. The place must be pulling as much power as a grow lab, but of course Shorty is off grid with an array of solar cells and wind turbines.

When Roz called, Polynesian music was playing loudly from home-made speakers in Shorty's sunroom. At a table overlooking the valley, sat the gangly octogenarian wearing magnifying goggles as he soldered two wires.

Shorty didn't hear the phone until the tenth ring. Then he turned and regarded it with magnified eyes. He blinked, tilted his goggles up, and answered it.

"Shorty."

"Hey, Shorty, I've got Pat for you," said Roz.

"You don't sound like Pat."

"I'm not. I'm Roz."

"I'm confused. Why would you say you're Pat then?"

"No—I—umh—"

In the reception at the hospital, Roz shook her head and looked to Pat for help. He spoke up. "Hey Shorty, it's Pat."

"Was that girl pretending to be you?"

Pat got straight to the point, "Shorty, we need your help."

"What can I do?"

Pat explained about the boat in the storm with the comms down. And how they wanted to use the radio station antenna to send a short-wave message to it.

"That's easy. I could call Darls at the station to set it up," said Shorty.

"Great idea, mate."

"You'll need to find me the call sign for the *Rainbow*."

"Onto it, mate. Thanks." Pat hung up.

CHAPTER FIFTY

BUNG

Bung's little house sits on the edge of the cliff at Anson Bay. The magnificent Pacific Ocean usually fills your view like you're standing on the shore. Which you are – just 100 metres straight upwards.

From Bung's big loungeroom windows there are usually only three things to see: green grass to the edge of the cliff; deep blue ocean to the horizon line; and light blue sky above that.

Three colours divided by two lines. Like a flag of three strips: sky blue; navy blue; and green.

Flag of the View from Bung's Loungeroom Windows

But now, Bung couldn't even see beyond the cliff. And he was looking. Standing at the big picture windows of his loungeroom holding a drink, Bung the ancient mariner stared into the clouds above his yard. He watched the rain lash the glass, and the wind assail the trees, and beyond that saw nothing but grey demons of tempest.

He'd just heard Darls's announcement on the radio. Now a hymn was playing. It melted his heart. It tingled his neck. It felt timeless, as if the ghosts of the past were standing there with him looking into the storm. Singing. Waiting. Praying. "God, please bring them home. God, please bring them home."

The phone rang. Bung caught it before the second ring, and said hello in Norf'lk language, "*Wataweih.*"

"Bung, it's Roz from the hospital."

"Hospital? What's wrong?"

"I've got Father Pat for you."

"What do I need a priest for?"

"No, it's nothing like that—umh—"

"Bung, it's Pat. What's the call signal for *Rainbow Warrior Six*?"

Bung recited the call signal: "UHZ seven two four." A direct answer to a direct question. Like he was back in the navy and had been asked for his serial number.

"Thanks mate. Stay on the line, Bung. We might need you again."

"Yes, sir."

There was a click and muzak filled the earpiece, but Bung held the receiver tight to his ear. Standing at attention. For news of his son. To be able to help. He would've waited there, holding that fucking muzak to his ear until his bones decayed. Until the marrow in his bones dried up, and his limbs slipped down and crumpled into a pile on the floor. Then he would've laid there on the ground holding that phone to his ear. Yes, sir. Until his fingers withered. Then he would've laid his head on the phone. And stared out the window and waited. Until his eyes dried out. Then he would've listened. And hoped. Yes, sir.

They say dogs are loyal. They ain't never seen a dad.

CHAPTER FIFTY-ONE
RECEPTION

In the waiting room, Roz, Mitch and Father Pat were hunched around the speakerphone.

In the radio studio, Darls bent over a comms box.

Everyone else on Norfolk Island listened to the four-part harmony singing the hymn on the radio. Many had hearts so full, tears overflowed from their eyes.

Outside, the wind tore at the sea and bent the pines and scared the palms. The sea and the sky were at war. And the *Rainbow Warrior VI* was somewhere in the middle.

CHAPTER FIFTY-TWO

BOAT

Annie slammed the lid closed with her left hand and clutched the safety lines with her right.

"Yay!" she screamed.

Charlie glanced over and yelled, "That's it!"

Annie held the safety lines close (and then far, and then close again, as her hand and the boat and everything in this wild wet world swayed).

What she saw was a two-metre, black plastic-coated, high-tensile wire with another wire coming off its middle. There were strong clips at all the three ends.

Annie couldn't figure it out, but initially imagined it was used to tie three people together. She held the ends apart, within the swaying world, with the storm screaming and everything banging, and the rain pellets drumming her jacket and echoing like a drum roll inside her hood.

"Three points of contact," Charlie yelled.

Annie looked at him, then back at the safety line, and repeated what she'd heard, "Three-person contact?"

She curled her lip and furrowed her brow. Then moved her head and squinted at the three clips and said, "Oh, I get it."

Then she advanced to the next challenge – crossing two metres of trampolining deck to reach Charlie.

CHAPTER FIFTY-THREE
STUDIO

The hymn finished and Darls spoke into the mic, "That was our very own, Choral Reefers, singing 'Brightly Beams'. Now, if you've just tuned in, we've got an emergency weather situation and all the comms are down. So, we're going to use some old-school technology to try to contact some friends who are out there in a boat in this mighty squall. I've got Shorty at the short-wave radio to talk me through it."

Darls flicked the mixer and said, "Hey, Shorty."

"Hey, Darls," came the voice from the speakers, "are you at the controls?"

"Yes, love," said Darls, "Walk me through it."

"OK," said Shorty. "From memory you've got an old Grundig, there in the studio."

Darls looked at the short-wave broadcasting equipment she'd never used before, and read the name aloud, "Eton. Elite 750?"

"Oh, they got a new one, eh?" said Shorty.

"I guess so," said Darls.

"OK, we'll muddle through it," said Shorty. "First find the power button."

In the Golden Orb café and the Olive Café, in Norfolk Mechanical and in Norfolk Telecom, business as usual was paused. Customers and staff alike were staring intently at the radio speakers, following the process in their imagination.

Even though none had ever seen the radio station's short-wave transmitter, they saw it in their heads. Hundreds of different versions.

Most residents knew Darls, but even the tourists who didn't know what she looked like, saw her crouched over the dials in a studio they'd never seen. They urged Shorty, whether they knew him or not, to instruct Darls properly and wisely, and quickly – because people they didn't know and who they suddenly cared for dearly – were at risk. They urged Darls to tweak the knobs to tune a broadcast for a separate frequency.

"Come on, Darls," they said to themselves.

"Come on, Shorty," they mouthed.

CHAPTER FIFTY-FOUR

BOAT

Annie was no longer terrified. She had her storm legs, and even though she was crouched down next to the box, her whole body moved like an accordion with the ups and down of gravity and with the furious forces pushing and pulling her from side to side.

She clenched the safety lines in her right hand and positioned that elbow along the box. Her left hand held the pole. Then she waited while the boat powered up another steep incline.

The pitch increased, triggering her vertigo. She shouldn't have looked back – *Jesus, Jesus, Jesus*. She shouldn't have looked back down towards the stern of the boat– *shit, shit, shit*. The whole world fell away, there, gaping down into a faraway ravine behind the boat. *Fuck, fuck, fuck* – it felt like she was being held by her legs from a ten-storey window. *Fuck, fuck, fuck*. She swung her head back to Charlie and saw the foaming crest ahead: *Fuck fuck fuck fuck. There's no way we're going to make it! We're going to flip.*

She fought her neck not to look back down aft again. Instead, Annie clenched her eyes and hot tears ran down her cold wet cheeks, and she lifted her hand and forced a quiet "Yahoo?" through her gritted teeth.

Feeble as it was, it did the job. It didn't quite flip the fear, but at least it turned the sticky edges.

The vessel somehow clung on and crunched over the unstable crest. And in that airborne second, Annie catapulted from her crevice, pulling hard with both arms, and slid across the deck to the pole behind Charlie; an impossible distance of two gigantic metres.

Charlie turned, smiled and nodded. Annie smiled victoriously. Then she looked at the safety lines in her hand and said, "Now that I've got it, I don't need it."

The outrageous punk gods of the ocean mosh-pit heaved the boat up; Annie, Charlie, and everything else not bolted down – including the Brown family – left the deck by 12 centimetres. Unfortunately, there was only 10 centimetres between Charlie's head and the fibreglass canopy of the wheelhouse.

Charlie's head smashed into the canopy. Then he and Annie, and everything else, smashed back to the deck.

Charlie said, "Put it on anyway." Then fell unconscious.

CHAPTER FIFTY-FIVE

TOWN

The machine-gun rain and howling wind ravaged the trees and the awnings and the garden furniture of Norfolk Island. But inside the cafés, shops, offices and homes, it couldn't be quieter. The only noise was Shorty talking to Darls quietly on the radio.

He gave the last instructions, then said, "OK, Darls. That should be it. You should be able to cross over to short wave, now."

"Fingers crossed," said Darls.

She actually did it. In the corner of the studio, in the little building under the huge antenna in the storm-blown paddock drenched with wet cows, Darls crossed her fingers. As did Pete in Pete's Place. As did Mitch, Pat, Roz, and Sarah and the other nurses. As did Sharyn and Monet and Danielle at Prinke. As did Mary and Tom-tom in her kitchen. In fact, about the only one who didn't cross his fingers, was Shorty.

For Shorty, if it didn't work, it had nothing to do with luck. It was just science. He'd done all he could. Crossing his fingers wouldn't help.

Darls came back on air, "Ok folks there'll be some dead air, now. But then, if we got this right, there should be static."

Shorty added, "That'll mean the transmitter's switched over to the short-wave band. Then we have to find our boat's frequency out there on the water."

"OK, here goes nothing," said Darls.

And there it was. Nothing.

All the radios, all over the island, suddenly went dead.

"Dead air" is the second worst sound a radio station can make. It causes a reflex in the listener to instinctively twirl the knob. Nature abhors a vacuum. But everyone, in every shop and office and house on Norfolk Island resisted that urge. Some twiddled their fingers, some turned the volume up. But they all listened to nothing.

The silence was deafening. You could almost hear the communal heartbeat pulsing in the ears of the entire island. Pulsing, pounding, a running-scared beat, like Bonzo drumming on Led Zepplin's "Black Dog".

Internal voices were screaming, urging, criticising, raging, praying, hoping.

Externally, brows furrowed, and frowns descended. Glances flicked from one person to another until the peak of anxiety — well beyond all reasonable tolerance of "dead air".

Then, reality dawned that the experiment hadn't worked. Mouths gaped and tears brimmed.

Then all the island's radios blared static.

The worst sound a radio station can make. Static. But people cheered. In the loungerooms and kitchens and cafés, all around Norfolk Island, in the middle of a storm, there was a cheer of relief.

A bray of joy roared from the houses and the shops, and all the cafés and hotels. Even from the hospital and from Daa Randa.

If anyone was outside on the streets they would've heard the communal joy over the storm. But no one was outside except the cows, who lifted their heads from chomping grass. They looked around for danger but soon got hungry and resumed their tireless labour.

CHAPTER FIFTY-SIX

BOAT

"Shit, shit, shit—fuck, fuck, fuck," said Annie to Charlie's inert body.

"Shit, shit, shit—fuck, fuck, fuck," she said to the wave breaking over their bow and pushing the boat starboard.

"Shit, shit, shit—fuck, fuck, fuck," she said to the suddenly spinning steering wheel.

Annie threw her hand out into the spinning wheel and caught it painfully on her wrist. The boat rocked.

Annie looked down at Charlie, who's head was bleeding: "What do I do now?"

She nudged him with her foot, "Are you dead? What do I do?"

"Hey, you!" she screamed at the cabin door, "Hey, arsehole! Come here. Now!"

CHAPTER FIFTY-SEVEN

BUNG

You know what Bung's doing.

Standing straight, with his lips pursed and a faraway look in his eyes. Holding the phone to his ear.

If you'd asked him at that moment to climb out of the trenches, over the dirt wall and charge into the enemy fire, he wouldn't have blinked. Wouldn't have gulped. Would've just nodded, "Yes, sir."

Would've breathed deeply for more air in his lungs, to enable him to run faster and hurt their bullets more. Would've moved his toes to activate his feet to hurdle higher over the rough ground, so they had to move their guns more. Flexed his shoulders to climb the trench faster and greet their fiery death faster. A sprinter on the blocks. Ready for anything. Anything. He'd do anything. Anything. Please. Sir. Anything. For. Charlie.

The phone clicked and Pat said, "Bung?"

"Yes, sir."

"You been listening?"

"Yes, sir."

"We're going to patch you through to Darls at the radio station."

"Yes, sir."

"You can walk her through the process of catching Charlie's frequency."

"Yes, sir."

"OK," said Pat, "You OK?"

"Yes, sir."

Standing there, in his loungeroom, bolt upright, his 75-year-old spine was arched and stacked, like a loaded bow. Chest out, stomach in, shoulders back. Drink in his left hand down by his side. Phone in his right hand up at his ear. Jaw strong. Face relaxed. Heart on fire.

Eyes staring through the windows at the clouds, at the enemy. Ready at a flinch to jump into that bastard and rip out its lungs. Straight through the glass. Straight out there, into the cloud and storm, to fight the sea and the sky, just to cause the slightest distraction on their attack on his son.

With the word, he would've gone straight over the cliff, just to ripple the water at the bottom, and give a millimetre of advantage to the *Rainbow Warrior VI* in its battle.

Yes, sir.

You know it.

CHAPTER FIFTY-EIGHT

RECEPTION

In the hospital reception, Father Pat talked into the speak-erphone while more people arrived from different parts of the hospital to watch and listen.

Closest to the phone were Roz, Mitch and Father Pat. Then there was Nurse Sarah and the other nurses, Dr Pete, and Bunny the chief gardener.

Then, in the outer ring were the psychologist, dentist, dental technician, plumber, Greg and Steve the ambos, all the kitchen and admin staff.

They could hear the radios from their offices, but it was the communal energy that drew them. Like in the old days when people used to gather around the radio in their living rooms. Except here, it felt more like a church service where people were gathered to pray.

On the phone was Darls in the studio, Shorty and Bung in their respective homes, and Henry "Weather Vane" Thompson at the meteorological station, whom Roz had called for an update.

Roz had acquitted herself as a radio producer. The reception where she worked had become the radio desk, while Darls and Shorty used the station equipment to perform the technical magic of simultaneously broadcasting two different wavelengths from a single antenna.

CHAPTER FIFTY-NINE
STUDIO

Darls was transmitting *Rainbow Warrior VI's* call signal, but there was nothing there. Only static. No one was picking up. Maybe the storm was interfering with the transmission. Maybe they'd capsized.

Sweat popped from Darls's forehead. "Shit, shit, shit," she said to the dial.

CHAPTER SIXTY

BOAT

"Shit, shit, shit," said Annie to a navigational screen that was beeping loudly and blinking red.

She looked up and saw the ocean, real and enormous and swallowing itself in humungous golf course-sized gulps. She was beyond terrified.

She knew the boat was moving differently. Lolling.

Before, steered by Charlie, it'd moved with intent. Erratically but with intent. Now it was listless and waiting to die.

Annie pushed the throttle and Charlie's body slid back along the deck and smacked into the transom.

"Oh fuck!"

The cabin door creaked open.

"You!" said Annie, glancing between ocean and Mr Brown whose sickly head nudged out of the crack in the hatch, "Come here. Quickly! Carefully! Now!"

"What?"

"Come here, now," yelled Annie. "And hold on! Quick."

She pushed the throttle and knew it was too fast compared with Charlie's driving. But she was too afraid to move the throttle back in case the boat stopped altogether.

Mr Hugh Brown, plastic surgeon, flew out the cabin hatch and slid along the aft deck, crashing into Charlie.

"Shit," said Annie.

She spun to see them clumped, sloshing across the deck together. Annie's temples pounded like bass drums about to explode from fear and pressure.

She looked at Mr Brown with the desperate eyes of a prisoner receiving a fatal injection and "Yahoo!" quivered from her tight white lips.

CHAPTER SIXTY-ONE

RECEPTION

Father Pat was talking on the speakerphone with Weather Vane, the meteorologist. It was being broadcast live.

The waiting room was deathly silent. The crowd were breathing quietly as they leaned forwards towards the reception desk, listening intently to the phone. Roz had turned off the main radio in the hospital because it had been causing feedback on air.

Weather Vane said, "This is known as a white squall. A sudden windstorm at sea."

"Different from a normal squall?" asked Father Pat.

"Yes. It doesn't have the normal black clouds associated with it, so you don't see it coming. It's just white clouds and a sudden increase in wind velocity. I think Polynesians know it as an Apū-hau. But because there's no black clouds we call it a 'white squall'. The only visible signs are big white-capped waves and broken water."

"So there's no warning if you're at sea?"

"Sadly, that's right, Father Pat."

There was pause as Father Pat gulped, then stammered and glanced around his neighbours. Roz stepped in, and said, "So—umh—what does it mean for us here on Norfolk Island, Vane?"

"Batten down the hatches, Roz. High winds. Heavy, slanted rain. Stay out of the water. Stay off the roads if you can."

"So, wherever you are now, stay there?" asked Father Pat.

"That's it. It won't be long. Short and sharp. But a potentially dangerous microburst. It'll be gone as quickly as it appeared. Get your emergency kit ready. Torch, supplies, fresh water, charge your electronic devices. Expect power outages. Clean the yard of anything not bolted down. Bring the pets inside and make sure everything's shut. Stay together and get the board games out."

"Thanks Vane."

"Welcome, Father Pat. Stay safe everyone."

"That was Henry Thomas, there, ladies and gents. Or, as we all know him, Weather Vane."

CHAPTER SIXTY-TWO

BOAT

"I can't," said Mr Hugh.

"You must," said Annie.

"No," said Mr Hugh.

"NOW!" ordered Annie, so loud, that Hugh's arms moved involuntarily and he started swimming up the deck like a frog.

It was a type of breaststroke, and the sort of thing you'd see dancers doing in a daggy 1940s musical, but here, on the toddler-pool deck, it made for surprisingly effective transit.

Annie threw the safety line back towards Hugh, breast-stroking up the aft deck and yelled, "Put it on."

The cable hit Hugh in the head and he screamed, "Ow!" and stopped swimming. Then the boat heeled and he slid back down the deck, thudding into Charlie.

Annie glanced back, did a double-take and yelled, "Put it on him, too."

Hugh wrapped himself around Charlie and started clipping wherever he could.

Ahead, the white mountain peaks were coming too fast, but Annie didn't dare pull the throttle back in case she lolled again.

They crashed up the outcrop of foam and the boat flicked upwards, driving vertical for a brief, breathless moment. Annie slammed against the pole behind her. Then the boat fell forward and, by the laws of physics, the surging wave kicked the hull and drove the boat straight ahead at shocking speed.

Like a stallion, it'd stood on its hind legs for a second before charging down the cliff.

Everything was merely hectic for a second, then the boat bottomed the trough of the wave, and everything flew forwards. Charlie and Hugh, tethered by wire, slid along the deck until their safety line wrapped around the pole causing the two men to slam into each other like clacker balls.

They knocked out Annie's legs on the way and she fell onto the beanbag of wet men, pulling the throttle back on the way.

The boat slowed.

Annie tried to climb to her feet, again, but instead only managed to twitch the throttle backwards again.

"Fuck fuck fuck," she swore repeatedly, and took all the gods' names in vain. Then she lifted her head above the dash at the wave coming at them.

Her eyes widened, trying to comprehend the physics. She'd never seen a wave like it. A freak of nature so monstrous, it was breathtaking. Annie gaped at it in awe. If it was a movie, it'd need an IMAX screen to grapple with its enormity. But it was real. They were sitting ducks. There was no way they'd make it. It was vertical. Like the scene in *Inception* when Leonardo DiCaprio folds the city up over itself, except here it's merciless nature at war, screaming at them, turning them and raining down torrents from a dam bursting on top of them. And coming at them. Fast!

The crest was so high, it disappeared above the wheel-house window, even though Annie was looking at it from low down, on her seat on top of Charlie.

It was going to pulverise them.

She jumped up and pushed the throttle full forward. The twin engines halted for a second that felt like a week.

Then it churned. Annie lowered her head and leaned into the wheel and pushed the throttle to the maximum of its housing, then kept pushing further – for no practical use, except pleading with the ghost in the machine to go faster. A guttural curse snarled from her clenched teeth, "Yaaaaaa-fuckin-hoooo."

Hugh Brown lifted his head from Charlie's armpit and looked out the wheelhouse window at certainty of death. His mouth opened to scream but no sound came out. He looked down at the dead man under him, the captain of the boat. Then up at the crazy woman who was probably about to kill him, who was muttering, "Yaaaa-fuckin-hoooo", as she pushed them all towards certain death. And he would've knocked her hand from the steering wheel if he wasn't so deathly feeble from dehydration. Instead, he slumped back into Charlie's armpit and hugged him.

CHAPTER SIXTY-THREE

RECEPTION

All those people in different uniforms standing around a priest talking into a phone – it looked like a Norman Rockwell painting.

Warm faces looking earnest, listening to an uplifting message by a seasoned pro.

Father Pat said into the phone, which was broadcast to the radios all over the island, "There'll be damage. But we'll lend a hand to fix it. Together. But people are harder to fix. So don't put yourself at risk. You're important to us. You're part of us. I'm thinking of Alice at Daa Randa."

And there she was chewing the Ferrero Rocher he'd given her, dribbling chocolate from the corners of her mouth.

"—And Sharyn and the ladies at Prinke. And Mary and George and Smiley."

And the boys at Slicks. I bet you're glad you got that extra generator now, fellas."

At the butcher shop, they raised a glass to the radio.

"—And Shorty down at 'Low Roof'. And Teddy and Rose, and Matt at 'Bigg Farm', who'll all be thinking about their crops."

On the balcony of the Bigg's homestead, overlooking the rows of lettuce, Teddy, Rose, Lee, Louci and Matt were sitting around a table, playing cards, listening to the radio. They all yelled "Yay!"

"You'll be right. There'll be a new harvest soon. Until then, we'll all have shredded lettuce. And Scoobie, who'll probably be up a pole fixing our electricity—"

Scoobie smiled at the radio as he drove home after being called out to fix a fallen power cable.

"And Nomes and the crew at the Olive, stay safe."

At the little café, all the staff were sitting around a table, sharing a meal and a drink, and they yelled, "Yay!"

"And Warren and Cynthia, our quiet achievers, who've planted thousands of native trees over the island."

In their bedroom in Anson Bay, the two septuagenarian lovers were lying in bed. They twinkled a smile at each other.

"And Ken and Margaret, and Kath, Anson, Cassie and Lilli and the rest of the lovely Christian family who, with the heart of kindness, teach us about community every day."

From the cliff at the end of Fisherman's Lane, a raucous cheer arose from the extended family of happy faces sitting around a long Norfolk pine table on a wide deck that'd weathered many such storms, "Yayyy!!!"

"And these wonderful folk, here, at the hospital. You should see 'em, Norfolk. Almost the entire staff of the hospital is crammed around us here in the waiting room. You've all been here, waiting to see a doctor, or a nurse.

And there's Nitin the dentist, Siebren the physio, Kate the psych.

"Now they're all here, in the waiting room. It's full to overflowing with familiar faces. People who've helped you many times. People who live to help. Admirable, eh? Warm cheery cheeks, all lively eyes and full hearts, because they're also hearing names of people they love. Family. It's the way it's always been here on Norfolk Island. And God willing always will be.

"Not many places have got what we have. Poor buggers. Cos it's the best thing in life, I reckon. A rare treasure. So hold it in your hearts now. And know you're part of it. Especially our guests, like Mitch, here. And Annie, his new wife, and that family of tourists on the boat. And our beloved Charlie. Each and every one of you. May God bless you all."

CHAPTER SIXTY-FOUR

BOAT

Without looking away from the screaming cliff of water that was about to smash them, Annie kicked at Hugh Brown, and said, "We're going uphill. You gotta wrap yourself around the pole the other way."

He groaned.

"Now!" she screamed.

He drowsily lifted his head and moved a listless arm towards the pole.

"Hurry! We've got seconds! Go, go, go," and she started kicking him.

"No, stop it," he said, suddenly alert, and fending her kicks.

"Go, go, go," said Annie and kept kicking him and nudging with her shoe, "Get around the pole. Get around the pole. Go, go, go."

Mr Brown squibbed away from her blows like an octopus. Not knowing where he was supposed to be going or why. Not trusting that it was for his own good. Merely avoiding the kicks.

He suckered over Charlie's body and then along the deck away from Annie. She used her foot to drag Charlie closer to her, on her side of the pole.

"Help," she said, "push him towards me. Now!"

And Hugh gave some sickly grunts and then slumped his face down onto the deck.

Still facing forwards and leaning into the wheel, Annie kept dancing her legs to move Charlie around to this side of the pole, so the safety line looped it.

And the boat started to climb.

And the mountain moved.

And the boat jumped a ripple of water the size of a tent.

And the twin engines roared out of the water before submerging and lurching the boat forwards. And everything slid backwards, and the engines dug in. And the wave attacked, trying to tip them back and take them all away. And Charlie started to slide backwards. And Hugh started to slide backwards.

Annie yelled at him, "Say 'yahoo', or we'll all die."

And Hugh grimaced at the crazy bitch killer, but the thought of his kids kicked him in the heart, and he forced it out: "Yahoo."

Annie urged the throttle but there was nowhere to push it. She feared she might break the stick but didn't want to let off.

There was nowhere to go. Nowhere to steer. Unless she wanted to turn and race down the cliff they'd already climbed. And she considered it but knew if she tried, they'd be sideways, and it'd scuttle them.

It was too late for anything else. They were past the point of no return. Nowhere to go, but up.

Nothing to do at the wheel, except hang on. Standing straight upright, in a boat ascending at 40 degrees and tilting. Standing at the wheel, the chair behind her, a pole behind that, a slick deck and sheer, monstrous, jaws of death behind that. She was a goner.

With nothing left to do, at the epicentre of desperation, Mitch filled her head. And love filled her heart. And tears filled her eyes. And in that moment – joy. And Annie thought she'd be OK to die. She'd loved. She'd been loved. Nothing was better. "Faaaarck," she screamed. "Yahoo," she shrieked. "Bring it on, you son of a bitch!"

The trajectory increased. The tethered men slid, back, along the deck. The cable connecting them caught around the pole behind Annie, and the inert bodies slowly bumped into one another.

Annie looked at them swishing together across the deck. She smiled because she had nothing better to do. Her fate was resigned. And she was slightly glad that life didn't stop being absurd all the way to the end.

She turned to face the Armageddon ahead. The boat climbed. The ocean rose. The deck tilted. The men banged into each other. Annie was forced backwards onto the cushioned seat of the captain's chair. *It's over now*, she thought, *may as well take a seat.*

A front-row seat for her own apocalypse. Outwardly, she watched the wave of mutilation sweeping over her. Inwardly, she thought of Mitch. And smiled.

Ain't love grand. A million songs, 100,000 fiction books, 10,000 sci-fi movies, and none can capture it adequately. None can define it. But we all know it.

Love.

It's all you need. Just the word says it all. Love. There's just degrees of it.

"I love you this much," she'd said to her mum with her arms spread.

"I love you to the moon and back," she'd said to her dad.

"Love you times infinity," she'd said to her best friend.

"Love you to unknown galaxies and back," she'd said to Mitch, her fellow Love Alien.

Annie remembered going to a space-themed fancy dress party when she was first dating Mitch. They didn't wear costumes but their friend, a gay Hare Krishna barber, Luna, brought along a roll of Alfoil because, he said, "Nothing says space like aluminium foil."

He made a hat for Annie and a silver glove for Mitch. Then he made himself a tinfoil skull cap with an antenna in the shape of a love heart on top.

"You're a Love Alien," Annie had told Luna.

Then Mitch had looked at Annie and said, "So are you."

They'd looked at each other for a heartbeat, then had their first kiss.

Seconds from death, and that's what she remembered. And her heart overflowed with love. Brimmed over with rosy tingles that blossomed all over her neck and chest, face and body.

CHAPTER SIXTY-FIVE

STUDIO

On the floor of the radio studio under the enormous antenna, Darls crouched down at a control box in the corner. She was holding headphones to her left ear and turning a dial slowly forwards and back with her right hand.

She was trying to connect with *Rainbow Warrior VI* using the call signal Bung had given her, but all she heard through the headphones was white noise.

"There! You got it," said Bung from a speaker in the announcer's panel.

"Sh-sh-shhhhh—" said Darls softly, as she leaned into the headphones and listened for something solid in the sea of stormy static. Like a safe cracker, she turned the dial in minute increments.

It should be right there, she thought. Then she looked away from the panel to check the co-ordinates Bung had given her, but just as she moved, she heard something.

Surely nothing. Surely, it was the movement of her head. But she swung back anyway.

It was a hollow of noise. The barest change of sound-wave. Not even a heartbeat. A bee's heartbeat.

As she listened, she realised she was crazy. There were a hundred sounds – white, grey and black – in the impenetrable fusion of static.

Nup. Nothing, she thought. *But it was right—about—*

Darls moved the dial one ridge of one fingerprint, and said aloud, "There."

And there was nothing. Just a different shade of grey of static. A slightly different shriek in the panic of white noise. She closed her eyes and focused her being into her ear and her right thumbprint.

Her mind moved into that space, like she was weaving between microscopic filaments in the panorama. Like focusing her third eye, she targeted the irregularity in the chaos and held her breath and zoned in. Then, she suddenly let go of the dial, like it was hot.

She played it for Bung, and said, "That's all we got, mate. It ain't it. But it's all there is."

"OK," said Bung.

Darls stood up and rubbed her stiff legs, then walked slowly to the desk and hooked into the broadcast from the reception at the hospital. She interrupted Pat's sermon, and said "Sorry Pat."

Pat said, on the radio, "Darls, what have you got, love?"

"Not much, I'm afraid, Pat," said Darls, "They're either not picking up, or—I don't know. I've drilled deep into the frequency for *Rainbow Warrior VI*, and this is all I've got."

She played the frequency so the whole island could listen to the static.

For three seconds.

For seven seconds.

For ten seconds.

For sixteen seconds.

"Just a bit longer," whispered Mitch. "Please."

Twenty-eight seconds ...

CHAPTER SIXTY-SIX

BOAT

Annie watched her death. Felt it eat her, in the wave that crashed over them and tilted the boat backwards.

She felt it. The emptiness. The sadness, the grief, the avalanche of feelings. And the panic rose to swallow her. And she whispered, "Mitch".

It brought him to mind, and in the storm of cold rain that'd been running down her numb face for an hour, she felt the blissful warmth of tears plopping out the corners of her eyes.

And little Annie huddled around her heart. Focused on it. And she felt closer to Mitch, now, than if she'd been standing next to him. Instead of here, lost on the sea in a boat about to die with two men shackled to her chair banging into each other on the deck.

A sound. She looked up to the radio when it made a sound. She saw a button. She pressed it.

CHAPTER SIXTY-SEVEN

WAITING ROOM

The static on the speakerphone cut to a different station of static. An impossible white noise of nature.

The squally sound of machine-gunned rain, smashed sideways by shrieking wind, with overtones of screaming motors, creaking wood, cracking fibreglass, and bending metal.

Everyone listening on Norfolk Island – which was everyone with working ears – noted the change in sound and gasped. But no one could comprehend the change, except Bung, who knew what it meant perfectly, and started dancing around his loungeroom.

Everyone else winced because the screaming was hard to hear. But they held their breath and listened to the static.

Then it said, "Hello?"

CHAPTER SIXTY-EIGHT

BOAT

As the boat tilted vertically, and Annie floated in that space before pain, she suddenly heard a different station of white noise.

The impossible white noise of hordes of humans, screaming in exaltation, "Yayyy!!!!!!!!" Echoing and distorting. She crinkled her brow and couldn't comprehend this box suddenly erupting into the sound of people cheering.

Then Mitch yelled, "Hello!"

CHAPTER SIXTY-NINE

WAITING ROOM

The box said, "Hello."

Mitch yelled, "Hello!"

The static said, "Mitch!"

Mitch said, "Annie!"

Annie's voice shouted over the radio, all over Norfolk Island, "Faaaarck I love you baby I'm gonna die. I love you so much. I love you so much. Is it really you or am I dead?"

In the reception area of the hospital, Mitch shouted, "I love you, too. You're alive. I love you so much—"

CHAPTER SEVENTY
BOAT

The engines screamed louder as they came out of the water. The boat screamed as it tilted beyond the vertical, to an angle no boat was meant to tilt. The sea screamed. Annie screamed. The men on the leash left the deck, and the family thumped into the cabin wall and in that moment ...

CHAPTER SEVENTY-ONE
THE MOMENT

A boat, vertical. Airborne. On the crest of a freak wave of a devastating white squall in the Pacific Ocean.

Held there, in that moment.

Two men tied together, hanging from a pole, suspended above the deck, hanging in space, above their own deaths.

A mother and her two teenage children, crushed against a marine ply hatch, in a cabin swimming with debris. Their three faces pressed together in a bubble outside the laws of gravity, marine biology and weather. A bubble of time where they have no control – where even fear is suspended – and all they have is that moment. Probably their last. And it's wild and it stretches, and it's silent and timeless. And it's destiny, waiting for the coin to land.

It's an island of 2,000 people, wide-eyed and wide-mouthed. Holding their communal breath, all focused on a radio, focused on a boat, focused on its tail on a wave bigger than a building. That moment is still. Calm. Peaceful.

It's like being an embryo. Where it's the sound of one, single, heart pound.

It's pure luck that any of us are alive at all. And we all know it.

It's a young newlywed, airborne, out of someone else's seat with salt water in her eyes, and droplets of whitewash in freeze-frame in front of her elated face, marvelling at the magic of it all. How all she wants is more, but is happy he's here with her, in her heart, in her ears, in this glinting crystalline moment. In death, she's happy.

Ain't love grand.

And finally, it's a bloke sitting in a wheelchair in a warm hospital on a small island with his heart 60 kilometres away, over mountainous seas, inside the chest of a woman, airborne, above someone else's seat on a boat. A beat. One, single heartbeat. Love.

It's a jackpot: falling in love. A double jackpot. You both have to win. Two, simultaneous jackpots.

Annie and Mitch weren't just lucky to have fallen in love with each other, got married, and gone on a honeymoon. They were stupendously, insanely, improbably, triple-simultaneous jackpot winners to have this moment.

"Happy honeymoon" the ocean god's punk kids whispered, as they surged under the tail of *Rainbow Warrior VI*, and wrecked the moment. They heaved and sent the boat over the crest and singing down the slope the killer wave. Sending the two men, the mother with her two kids, and the airborne woman, all crashing in the opposite direction with bloody force.

"Yayyyy," Annie screamed.

And "Yay," came the chorus from the listeners all over the island.

And "Yay," came through the boat's radio from the chorus of people packed into the hospital reception.

Annie talked quickly because she was grateful to have breath enough to speak now, before the next wave inevitably took her, "Love, I love you!" she yelled, "I love you. I love you."

Mitch's voice came from the radio, "Love, I love you, too! I love you."

Ain't love grand.

Love. None of us can explain it. But we all know what it is. And sometimes it's all you can say, "I love you," because it means everything. There's just degrees of it.

Annie said, "Love, I love you so much."

Mitch: "I love you so much."

Annie: "I love you more."

Mitch: "Love Alien, I love you to the galaxies and back."

Annie: "How did you get me?"

Mitch: "Ham radio."

"You freak," Annie laughed. Then went silent.

Raging storm filled the airwaves. Crashing waves and screaming blue nature. Everyone thought they'd lost her. Mitch said, "Annie?"

Annie swallowed her tears enough to talk, "Darling, it's fucked," she said. "The ocean turned squall and Charlie's down. He hit his head. And I don't know how to drive this thing. Oh God, I want to see you so much. Oh God, I want to see you so much but I'm gonna die." She shrieked and everyone knew they were her last words.

Everyone except Mitch, who yelled, "No, no, no. No, love! You're gonna be OK. We got Bung on the line."

"Who?"

"Put him through, Roz," said Mitch.

Roz switched lines. Bung came on the speakerphone and on the radios in the convenience store and the government office, and in the petrol station and in all the houses where ears were wrapped, and Norfolk was rapt.

And also out on the fishing boat, *Rainbow Warrior VI*, named after *Rainbow Warrior V*, after *Rainbow Warrior IV*, after *Rainbow Warrior III*, and after *Rainbow Warrior II*, which Bung had named after the Greenpeace vessel *Rainbow Warrior* that was sunk by French saboteurs in 1985. But there's no time for that story, people's lives are at stake.

"I'm Bung, Charlie's father."

"Hi Bung, I'm Annie. I'm sorry he's—Oh, God, the wave's so big, Bung."

"Keep calm, Annie. Breath, girl."

"Breathe!? I keep going up these mountain waves. They're going to flip me."

"OK you're buggered. Take a deep breath. Now. Do exactly what I say, sailor. Got it?"

"Yes, Bung."

"Breathe," he said, "Now."

Annie forced a breath; it felt like the first one she'd breathed in long time.

"OK," she said.

"OK, now, where are you on the wave?"

"At the bottom."

"OK, throttle?"

"Full forward."

"OK, ease it back to half."

Annie slowly moved the throttle back to halfway, "Done."

"And steer starb—steer left a bit. Just a bit, half a turn. We want to slow your ascent. Give us some time. OK?"

"OK."

"Done that?"

"Yes, Bung."

"Good work. State of the boat?"

Annie looked around and said, "Intact. A lot of water on the deck."

"Yep, she's a good 'un. She'll get you home."

"I'm so scared," Annie started to cry.

"Breathe, sailor."

"Yes, Bung," she snivelled.

"State of the crew?"

"Charlie down, bleeding from a head wound. Tied by safety line around this chair to Mr Arsehole."

"Who?"

"Oh, I—um—don't know his real name. They took our Airbnb and didn't—Anyway, I didn't know how to tie them together, but he's probably OK. The rest of the family, wife, two kids, in cabin, seasick. Can't see them. Everyone's got jackets on."

"Good work. How's that wave looking?"

"Oh—so fuckin' big. Big and rough and fast. And huge. Should I turn around?"

"No, Annie. You can't outrun it. Just find a sweet spot—feel with your hand on the throttle—" Bung explained about steering through rough weather while everyone on Norfolk Island listened, urging the boat to get through the next monster wave.

Bung instructed Annie to ensure the radio beacon was on. He talked her through the next monster, and the next one. Behind her, Charlie groaned.

"He's alive! Charlie! Charlie!" said Annie.

"Come on, boy-o," said Bung. "Up yorle get, Charlie. We need yorle, now."

"Oi," said Charlie. Carefully, he lifted himself onto his elbows and tried to pull himself up but realised he was tied around the pole to Mr Hugh Brown, who was lying on the wet deck looking up at Charlie mournfully. It seemed like the only parts of Mr Hugh that could move were his yellow eyes.

Charlie said, "What the—?" He held his head, "Ow," and looked around at the warring sea. "Faaaaaarck!"

Bung's voice came from the radio, "Charlie?"

"Dad?" said Charlie and looked at the radio and yelled, "Is that you?"

"Yeah, boy," said the radio. "Can you help this lady?"

Charlie moved his head as far as the line would allow so he could see Annie at the wheel. "She's doing good, dad. A bit more throttle, Annie."

Hugging the pole, Charlie lifted himself onto one knee, and peered around the chair to see better, and said, "A bit left, love. Steer. Yep, that's it. Good."

He untangled himself from Hugh Brown, clipping the inert body to the pole and the gunwale. Then he stood up properly, reaching for the wheel.

"I've got the wheel, dad," said Charlie. "Annie's done great. We're coming home. Have services ready, please. Twenty minutes. We're low on gas. It's gonna be close."

Suddenly, in the waiting room and all the other rooms, all over the island, people clicked into action.

Father Pat got Roz's attention, who opened the line.

"Not everyone," said Father Pat over the radio. "OK everyone, wait a sec. Remember we got severe weather. I know you'll be hoping to lend a hand. Tom. Johnno. Duffy. I know you, Tet, you'll be out of your seat."

And they were – halfway to standing, caught there, by Father Pat's voice, "But we've got enough people out there already. We've got professionals. We've got Ben from the firies. Alexei at the police. Greg and Steve, the ambos. I'm looking at 'em. They're ready to go. The lighter boys will be down there for the crane. But that's enough, eh."

But all around the island, people edged toward their doors, as if playing that kids' game "Statues" where you have to freeze until you think they're not looking, then inch forwards.

Except Mitch, who wheeled himself out from the desk.

"Excuse me, Pat," he said to Pat who was blocking his way.

"Oh, heaven help me," said Pat, forgetting he was being broadcast. "You again."

Mitch raised his eyebrows and motioned with his head for Pat to move.

"There'll be no stopping you, I imagine," said Father Pat.

"Nope."

Pat shook his head and exhaled frustration, then said, "Alright then, see you all at the docks. But! Please, be careful!"

CHAPTER SEVENTY-TWO

TOWN

The exodus was momentous. A convoy of headlights, led by the flashing lights of the emergency vehicles, threaded a weaving line down the switchback roads of the pitch-black hills to Kingston's pier.

CHAPTER SEVENTY-THREE

KINGSTON PIER

Every shape of car and truck was parked on the hill overlooking the pier. They all struck their high beams and lit up the scene.

There were only five vehicles on the pier itself. The police car, the ambulance, and a fire engine, all with lights flashing. There was also Bung in his truck. And Father Pat's old truck with Mitch sitting in the passenger seat.

There was nothing but oblique fog with headlights cutting into it and flashing emergency lights bouncing off it in red, blue and yellow.

The storm yelled a monotonous threat. Wait. The war of crashing waves. Wait. The flashing lights bouncing. Wait. And slowly emerging, a red and green apparition. It appeared then disappeared in the waves and fog.

The *Rainbow Warrior VI* limped around the head of the pier. The crowd cheered her in. Horns were playing a crazy rendition of "Welcome Home Sailor from the Sea."

Emergency services caught her stern, tied her up and climbed aboard. First, they brought the Brown family off the boat. Then they brought Charlie and Annie off.

Annie was wrapped in a silver thermal blanket; Mitch tried to get out of his seat, but Pat said, "Wait," and he came around and helped him out of the truck. Then Pat was under Mitch's arm helping him limp towards Annie, who was being helped by Greg and Steve.

In the misty spotlight, the lovers went to each other and hugged in the rain while Pat held an umbrella above them. As they hugged, the chorus of horns blasted a riot.

CHAPTER SEVENTY-FOUR

WARD

Twenty minutes later, the hospital ward was crowded with nurses, doctors, ambos, police, and Father Pat. Every bed in the hospital had been pressed into action.

The sick and bruised Brown family – Hugh, Marjory, Brooklyn and Hugh Junior – were in beds. Charlie was in a bed with Bung standing next to him. And Annie and Mitch were in neighbouring beds. Other onlookers were standing around and peering in from the door.

Dr Pete shooed them away, "It ain't a cinema. Go on. Go home. And don't have a bloody accident."

Nurse Sarah pushed Annie's bed together with Mitch's. Then she closed the plastic curtain around them.

Mitch whispered, "I love you."

Annie whispered, "I love you more."

Mitch laughed and said, "Impossible."

Annie said, "Anything's possible, my love."

Mitch said, "Maybe we should stay in hospital together. I spend most of my time here."

"No, I wanna get you home to Mary's and look after you."

"Home."

"What?"

"You said 'home'."

They beamed into each other's eyes.

"Forged in the fire we are."

They laughed tears. "One week married and we found our family."

"We found our home."

CHAPTER SEVENTY-FIVE

OCEAN VALLEY

Three months later, on a tiny green island in the enormous blue Pacific, on the sandy shore, where a valley of pines rolled out from Mary's yard and touched the sea below Bung's home.

There was a large working-bee of people gathered in ocean valley. Annie and Mitch were there. Bung and Charlie were there. Mary, George, Smiley, Tom-tom and Bluey were there. Father Pat was there. George the administrator, Susan the photographer, Allison from the website, and Darls from the radio were there. Even some people who actually knew how to construct an aquaculture plant were there, too.

A shovel was held. A plot was turned. Photos were taken. And building began on PaciFolk Aquaculture.

There were numerous amazing disruptions in construction.

ACKNOWLEDGMENTS

Thank you to the Norfolk Island Language Commission "Dictionary Project" for their kind assistance in translating my English dialogue into Norfolk Island language. The spelling provided by the NILC is based on their work to date, and the final version of the dictionary may be subject to change. The Norfolk Island Language Commission is a sub-committee of the Norfolk Island Council of Elders.

My thanks to Lucy Powis for taking me swimming each day and for holding my arm every step of the way through this book; to Susan Prior my superb editor, who makes sentences make sense; to John and Annie Kenny, for your legal and publishing guidance and relentless enthusiasm; and to Emily Bay, for your divine inspiration. Thanks also to my eternal cheer-readers, Andrew Dib and Kate Foote; to Rob Mort the genius of aquaculture, for advice on fish farms; to John Leighton and the Scroll Writers Group, for reading and listening; to D&SE for life and soul; and to Candice, for veterinary expertise.

My thanks also to everyone in the book, for being such a lovely part of my life here on Norfolk Island, and for welcoming me into yours. My apologies to all those wonderful characters I left out, who are such a rich part of the unique Norfolk Island community. Prinke.

Thank you, John and Denise, and the rest of the fam. As always.

CREDITS

AUDIO

"Stardust"; writer Carmichael, H., Parish, M. (1927); performer Nat King Cole; album *Love is the Thing* (1957); producer Lee Gillette; Capitol Records.

"Fly Me to the Moon", writer Howard, B. (1954); performer Frank Sinatra; album *It Might as Well Be Swing* (1964); producer Sonny Burke; Decca Records.

"Intergalactic", writers Diamond, M., Horovitz, A., Yauch, A., Caldato, Jr., M. (1998); performers The Beastie Boys; album *Hello Nasty* (1998); producers Beastie Boys, Mario Caldato Jr; Grand Royal / Capitol Records.

"Satellite of Love", writer Reed, L. (1970); performer Lou Reed; album *Transformer* (1973); producers Bowie, D., Ronson, M.; RCA records.

"Space Oddity", writer Bowie, D. (1969); performer David Bowie; album *David Bowie (Space Oddity)* (1969); producers Dudgeon, G., Visconti, T.; RCA Records.

"Starman", "Soul Love", "Moonage Daydream", "Ziggy Stardust and the Spiders from Mars", writer Bowie, D. (1969-71); performer David Bowie; album *The Rise and Fall of Ziggy Stardust and the Spiders from Mars* (1972); producers Scott, K., Bowie, D.; RCA Records.

"Life on Mars", writer Bowie, D (1971); performer David Bowie; album *Hunky Dory* (1971); producers Scott, K., Bowie, D.; RCA Records.

"The Man Who Sold the World", writer Bowie, D (1970); performer David Bowie; album *The Man Who Sold the World* (1970); producer Visconti, T.; Mercury Records.

"Every 1's a Winner", writer Brown, E (1978); performers Hot Chocolate; album *Every 1's a Winner* (1978); producer Most, M.; RAK Records.

"Bad Moon Rising", writer Fogerty, J.; performers Creedence Clearwater Revival; album *Green River* (1969); producer Fogerty, J.; Fantasy Records.

"My Island Home", writer Murray, N (1986); performers Warumpi Band; album *Go Bush!* (1987); producers Murray, N. and Price, D.; Parole Records; performer Christine Anu; album *Stylin' Up* (1995); producer Bridie, D.; White Label Records / Mushroom.

"Stayin' Alive", writers Gibb, B., Gibb, R., Gibb, M. (1977); performers Bee Gees; album *Saturday Night Fever* (1977); producers Bee Gees, Galuten, A., Richardson, K.; RSO Records.

"Cancer", writers Cook, P., Moore, D.; performers Derek and Clive; album *Derek and Clive (Live)*; Island Records.

"A Hard Rain's a-Gonna Fall", writer Dylan, B. (1962); album *The Freewheelin' Bob Dylan* (1963); producer Hammond, J.; Columbia Records; performer Bryan Ferry;

album *These Foolish Things* (1973); producers Ferry, B., Porter, J., Punter, J.; Island Records.

MOVIES

The Man Who Fell to Earth (1976); director Nicolas Roeg; cast David Bowie, Rip Torn; British Lion Films.

Moulin Rouge (2001); director Baz Luhrmann; cast Nicole Kidman, Ewan McGregor; 20th Century Fox.

Saturday Night Fever (1977); director John Badham; cast John Travolta, Karen Gorney; Paramount Pictures.

Xanadu (1980); director Robert Greenwald; cast Olivia Newton-John, Gene Kelly; Universal Pictures.

Royal Wedding (1951); director Stanley Donen; cast Fred Astaire, Jane Powell; Metro-Goldwyn-Mayer.

ENTITIES

Radio Norfolk is a government-owned, government-run radio station servicing Norfolk Island on 89.9FM and 1566AM. The island's other two local stations are *87.6 FM Norfolk Island*, owned by the Bounty Folk Museum, and the community radio station, *90.9 Pines FM*.

Norfolk Island Health and Residential Aged Care Service (NIHRACS) delivers healthcare to the Norfolk Island community and its visitors, with: 24/7 Emergency Department; In patient and support services; GP Clinic; Dental Clinic; Allied Health; Residential Aged Care services; Home Care services in partnership with Care Norfolk.